"It is by no means unusual for journalists of both sexes to invade my beach, nor for young women to arrange to be stranded there."

"In the hope that you'll come to the rescue?"

"Their hopes are usually higher—or lower—than that," said Luke, his mouth twisting in distaste. "I do not," he added sardonically, "delude myself that women are attracted to me in person. Only to my money."

"And the power you used to amass it. Isn't power supposed to be the ultimate aphrodisiac?" Isobel smiled politely. "You Greeks have a word for everything."

Luke inclined his head. "The rest of the world owes a lot to us."

"What happens to trespassers when you're not here?"

"My security deals with them. You would have been removed before I arrived."

"Which would have saved a lot of trouble." One way or another.

Luke gave her the unsettling smile again. "But it would also have deprived me of the pleasure of meeting you."

CATHERINE GEORGE was born on the border between Wales and England, in a village blessed with both a public and a lending library. Fervently encouraged by a like-minded mother, she early developed an addiction to reading.

At eighteen Catherine met her husband, who eventually took her off to Brazil. He worked as chief engineer of a large gold-mining operation in Minas Gerais, which provided a popular background for several of Catherine's early novels.

After nine happy years, the education of their small son took them back to Britain, and soon afterward a daughter was born. But Catherine always found time to read, if only in the bath! When her husband's job took him abroad again she enrolled in a creative writing course, then read countless novels by Harlequin authors before trying a hand at one herself. Her first effort was not only accepted, but voted best of its genre for that year.

Catherine has written more than sixty novels since, and she won another award along the way. But now she has come full circle. After living in Brazil, and in England's the Wirral, Warwick and the Forest of Dean, Catherine now resides in the beautiful Welsh Marches—with access to a county library, several bookshops and a busy market hall with a treasure trove of secondhand paperbacks!

THE POWER OF THE LEGENDARY GREEK
CATHERINE GEORGE

~ The Greek Tycoons ~

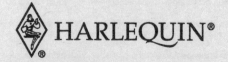

HARLEQUIN®

TORONTO • NEW YORK • LONDON
AMSTERDAM • PARIS • SYDNEY • HAMBURG
STOCKHOLM • ATHENS • TOKYO • MILAN • MADRID
PRAGUE • WARSAW • BUDAPEST • AUCKLAND

Recycling programs
for this product may
not exist in your area.

ISBN-13: 978-0-373-52770-0

THE POWER OF THE LEGENDARY GREEK

First North American Publication 2010.

Copyright © 2010 by Catherine George.

Printed in U.S.A.

THE POWER OF THE
LEGENDARY GREEK

PROLOGUE

HE STRODE along the top floor of the building towards the double doors standing open at the far end, savouring the moment as he entered the room to smiles of welcome from eleven members of the board. The twelfth member, the only woman present, speared him with eyes like shards of black jet as he gave her a formal bow. The tall windows looked out on a panoramic view of Athens, but inside the boardroom all eyes were riveted on his face as he took the only empty chair and sat, composed, to open his briefcase.

The woman at the head of the table watched his every move like a cat ready to pounce on its prey, but Luke ignored her, supremely confident of success. Due to weeks of secret negotiations held with every man in the room, the meeting today was a mere formality. Once formal greetings were concluded, Luke got to his feet to outline details of his proposal, ignoring the mounting fury of the woman as he brought his bid to a conclusion.

He scanned each face in turn.

'All those in favour?'

Every hand but one shot up in instant approval as Melina Andreadis surged to her feet in furious dissent. Dressed in stark couture black, her signature mane of ringlets rioting in cruelly youthful contrast around her ageing face, she directed a look of such venom at her adversary he should have turned to stone where he stood.

She swept the basilisk stare over every man at the table. 'You fools think you can turn my company over to this—this playboy?' she shouted, incensed, and shook her fist at the man unmoved by her tirade. 'I vote *against*! I refuse to allow this.'

Luke stared her down, his face blank as a Greek theatre mask to hide the triumph surging through his veins. 'It is already done. My more than generous terms are accepted by the Board by majority vote.'

'They cannot do this. I forbid it. This is *my* airline,' she hissed, enraged.

His eyes glittered coldly as they speared hers. 'No, *kyria*. It *was* my grandfather's airline, never yours. And now it is mine. I, Lukas Andreadis, own it by right of purchase—and of blood.'

CHAPTER ONE

THE smudge on the horizon gradually transformed into an island which surged up, pine-clad, from the dazzling blue sea. As the charter boat grew nearer, Isobel could see tavernas with coloured awnings lining the waterfront, and houses with cinnamon roofs and icing-white walls, stacked like children's building blocks on the slopes above. She scanned the houses as the boat nosed into the harbour, trying to locate the apartments shown in her brochure, but gave up, amused, when she saw that most of them had the blue doors and balconies she was looking for. She hoisted her backpack as the boat docked and picked up her bags with a sigh of relief. She'd arrived!

Isobel's first priorities were lunch and directions to her holiday apartment on this picture-perfect island of Chyros. The taverna her brochure indicated for both was inviting and lively, its tables crammed inside and out with people eating, drinking and talking non-stop. She made a beeline for one of the last unoccupied tables under the awning outside, and tucked her bags close to her feet as she sat to study the menu. With a polite '*parakalo*,' she pointed out her choice to a waiter and was quickly provided with mineral water and bread, followed by a colourful Greek salad with feta cheese. She fell on the food as though she hadn't eaten for days; which wasn't far off the truth. She enjoyed the arrival part of holidays a whole lot more than the travelling.

'You enjoyed the *salata*?' asked the waiter, eyeing her empty plate in approval.

Isobel smiled, delighted to hear English. 'Very much; it was delicious.' She produced her brochure. 'Could you help me, please? I was told I could collect the keys to one of these apartments here.'

He nodded, smiling. 'My father has keys. He owns the Kalypso. Wait a little and I take you there.'

Isobel shook her head, embarrassed. 'That's very kind of you, but I can't interrupt your work. I can take a taxi—'

He grinned. 'My father is Nikos, also owner of the taverna. He will be pleased if I take you. I am just home from the hospital.'

She eyed the muscular young man in surprise. 'You've been ill?'

'No. I work there. I am a doctor. But at home I help when we are busy. I am Alex Nicolaides. If you give me your name for my father, I take you to the Kalypso.'

She told him she was Isobel James and, by the time she'd downed more water and paid the bill, the helpful Alex was on hand again.

'It is near enough to walk,' he informed her and picked up her luggage, but Isobel hung on to the backpack.

'I'll take this.'

'It has your valuables?' he asked as they walked along the marina.

'In a way.' She pulled the peak of her cap down to meet her sunglasses. 'Some of my drawing materials.'

'You are artist, Miss James?'

Isobel smiled. 'I try to be.'

Her escort was right. It was not far to the Kalypso holiday

lets, but in the scorching sunshine it was far enough for Isobel to feel very hot and travel-weary by the time they reached a group of six white cottages scattered on the hillside on the far side of the waterfront. Offset at different angles amongst the greenery, all of them had blue-painted balconies overlooking the boats bobbing on the brilliant waters below.

Her guide checked the number on Isobel's key tag and eyed her doubtfully. 'Your house is last, high on hill. You will not be lonely?'

She shook her head. Far from it. The peace and semi-isolation of the cottage was exactly what she needed.

The other houses had been left quite a distance behind by the time the young man led the way up a steep path quilted with soft, slippery pine needles. He put the bags down on a veranda furnished with reclining chairs and a table, and with a flourish unlocked the door of Isobel's holiday home.

'Welcome to Chyros, Miss James; enjoy your stay.'

She turned from the view. 'I'm sure I will. One last thing—where exactly is the nearest beach?'

'Next to the harbour. But down here is one you will like better.' He pointed to a path among the Aleppo pines behind the house. 'Smaller, very pretty, and not many people because the path is steep.'

'Sounds wonderful. Thank you so much for your help.' Isobel gave him a warm smile as she said goodbye and went inside to inspect her new quarters, which consisted mainly of one big air-conditioned room with a white-tiled floor and yellow-painted walls. It was simply furnished with a sky-blue sofa and curtains, two white-covered beds and a wardrobe; and through an archway at the end a small kitchen and adjoining bathroom. Everything was so scrupulously clean and peaceful it felt like sanctuary to Isobel.

Her friend Joanna, her regular holiday companion in the past before her marriage, had disapproved of Isobel's choice and had urged her to stay at a hotel on somewhere lively like glitzy Mykonos. But Isobel had opted for quiet, idyllic Chyros, where she could paint, or do nothing at all for the entire holiday, with no demands on her time. Or her emotions.

Isobel unpacked, took a quick shower and, cool in halter neck and shorts, went outside on the balcony. She sent a text to Joanna to report safe arrival and sat down with her guide-book, hair spread out on a towel over her shoulders to dry a little in the warm air before she set about taming it. A fan of Greek mythology from the time she could first read, she checked the location of the island of Serifos, where legend said Perseus and his mother Danae had been washed ashore in a chest set adrift on the sea, but decided the journey there could wait until she'd recovered from this one.

Isobel sat back, content to do nothing at all for a while, but in the end balanced a pad on her knee as usual and began to sketch the boats in the harbour below. Absorbed, she went on working until the light began to fade and sat up, yawning, too tired to go back down to the taverna for supper. Instead, she would eat bread, cheese and tomatoes from the starter pack of supplies provided with the cottage, then, with her iPod and a book for company, she would go early to bed. Tomorrow, as Scarlett O'Hara said, was another day.

Isobel lingered on the veranda as lights came on in the boats far below, and in the houses climbing the slopes above them. Music and cooking smells came drifting up on the night air as she leaned back in her chair to watch the stars appearing like diamonds strung across the dark velvet sky. Contrary to Joanna's worried forecast, she felt peaceful rather than lonely. For the first time in weeks she was free of the dark cloud she had been unable to shake off, no matter how hard she worked. And there had to be something really special in the air here, because she felt sleepy, even this early. It would be no hardship to go to bed.

She woke early next morning, triumphant to find she'd not only fallen asleep easily, but passed the entire night without a bad dream to jolt her awake in the small hours.

After breakfast Isobel dressed in jeans and T-shirt over a pink bikini, pulled her hair through the back of a blue baseball cap and set out in the cool morning air to find her way back down to the harbour. She strolled past the boats on the waterfront and then turned up towards the town square, returning friendly smiles from ladies in black and from old men already seated outside their doors. She found a little kiosk-type corner shop already open and bought postcards, bread, mineral water and luscious grapes, then retraced her route back to the cottage. Finally, armed with sunglasses and a few basic necessities in her backpack, Isobel set off on the path recommended by Alex Nicolaides.

He was right. It was steep enough to make the descent downright scary in places. But the beach, deserted and utterly beautiful, was well worth the effort when she finally arrived, panting, on the bone-white shingle edging the crescent of sand. Isobel gazed, entranced, itching for paint to capture the way the sea shaded in jewel colours from pale peridot-green, through aquamarine and turquoise into a deep celestial blue. Greenery grew surprisingly close to the water's edge, with tamarisk and something she thought might be juniper among the pines and aromatic maquis-type vegetation. She sighed, frustrated, as a salt breeze rustled the pines. The scene cried out for watercolour. But getting the necessary materials down that path would be tricky. For now she would settle for just sketching it. Isobel chose the nearest rock formation as a base, took off her jeans and shirt, slathered herself in suncream, then pulled the peak of her cap down low, settled herself on a towel with her backpack to cushion her against the rock and began to draw.

No one climbed down the path to join her, but after an hour or so of perfect peace, small boats began discharging passengers at intervals and soon there were people sunbathing and picnicking, and children playing ball, shrieking joyfully as they ran in and out of the sea. So much for peace and quiet. Smiling philosophically, Isobel braced herself for the climb up the cliff to go in search of an early lunch. But while she gathered up her belongings she spotted a gap in the rocks on the far side of the beach and couldn't resist strolling over to investigate. On closer inspection, the fissure was very narrow and dark with overhanging shrubbery. But, by taking off her backpack and hugging it to her chest, she could just manage to squeeze along the rocky passage, which narrowed so sharply at one point Isobel almost gave up. But when the passage widened again curiosity propelled her forward, her sneakers slipping slightly on the wet rock as she emerged at last into a much smaller cove sheltered by high, steep cliffs. With not a soul in sight.

Isobel surveyed her deserted paradise in delight. She would make do with grapes and water for lunch, right here. She stripped down to her bikini again and settled under the overhang of a rock formation shaped so much like a rampant lion she promised herself to sketch it later. She drank some water, nibbled on her grapes, then took off her cap and moved further into the shade of the rock to catnap.

But her newfound peace was soon shattered by the roar of some kind of engine. Basic survival instinct sent Isobel scrambling up on to the steep rock as a man on a Jet Ski shot straight towards her. At the very last minute he veered away, laughing his head off as he went speeding out to sea again. Heart hammering, Isobel cursed the idiot volubly, so furious she lost her footing as she turned to jump down and flailed wildly to avoid falling, her scream cut off as her head met rock with a sickening crack that turned the world black.

Lukas Andreadis was looking forward to a swim followed by a good dinner and an entire evening with no discussion of takeovers, air travel, shipping, or any other form of transport. After working towards it all his adult life, he would celebrate his triumphant defeat of Melina Andreadis alone, in the place he loved best. He began to relax as the helicopter flew over familiar blue waters. When the island finally came into view his spirits rose as usual at the mere sight of Chyros, which stood for peace and privacy in a life which held precious little of either back in Athens. But, as he took the helicopter low on its descent to the villa, Luke cursed in angry frustration. A naked female was sunbathing on his private beach. Again.

He set the machine down on the helipad at the back of the house, switched off the engine and jumped out, crouching low until he was free of the rotating blades. He hurried past the pool to make for the trees lining the cliff edge, and scowled down at the figure lying motionless far below. Why, in the name of all the gods, couldn't they leave him alone? He turned as his faithful Spiro came rushing to greet him, and exchanged affectionate greetings before pointing down at the beach.

'Someone down in the cove again. Where the devil is Milos?'

'He needed time off. Shall I take the boat?'

'No; leave it to me.' Luke collected his bags and strode past the palms and oleanders in the lush garden. Instead of going through his usual ritual of breathing in the peace and welcome of his retreat, he raced up the curving staircase, threw off his clothes, and pulled on shorts and T-shirt, thrust bare feet into deck shoes, smiling in reassurance at Spiro as the man began to unpack. 'Don't worry, I won't hurt the woman.'

'I know that!' retorted the man, with the familiarity of one who'd known—and loved—his employer from birth. 'Wear your dark glasses—and don't drive too fast.'

Luke Andreadis collected two sets of keys, stopped in the kitchen for an affectionate greeting with Eleni, Spiro's wife, then checked again from the cliff edge, his face grim when he saw the prone figure still frying down on the beach. The stupid woman was risking a bad case of sunstroke at the very least—but not for long.

He ran back through the garden, vaulted into the jeep parked behind the villa and drove up the cypress-lined drive and out on to the road, taking the twists and turns of the tortuous descent at a speed which would have given Spiro a heart attack. Forced to slow down as he reached the town, Luke drove more circumspectly through the main square and on past the tavernas and coffee shops on the waterfront, then parked well out of sight at his secluded private mooring at the far end. He leapt onto the deck of the *Athena*, cast off and switched on the engine and, once clear of the marina, sped across the water past the crowded beach and round the cliffs to his private cove. He moored the boat at a jetty hidden among the rocks, his eyes smouldering. The woman was still there.

'You're trespassing,' he bellowed, storming across the shingle. But as he reached her he realised that the woman was unconscious. Sprawled at an awkward angle, she lay face down and utterly still, a mass of long fair curls streaming over her shoulders. He reached up to turn her face towards him, but dropped his hand when she opened pain-filled blue eyes which darkened in terror at the look of menace on the face close to hers.

'You had a fall. What are you doing here?' he demanded.

'Sorry—don't understand,' she said faintly, shrinking from him, then stifled a moan, her face screwed up in pain as she tried to back away.

'You fell. Your head is injured,' he said in English, cursing silently as her move brought blood trickling from a gash on her temple.

'Ankle, too.' She swallowed painfully. 'I slipped when you came roaring out of the sea at me on that Jet Ski—'

'Jet Ski?' Luke glared at her. 'You are delirious from your fall, *kyria*. I do not own such a thing. I came by boat.' Scowling, he examined the foot wedged tightly in a crack in the rock. 'I must pull it out. But it will hurt.'

She clenched her jaw stoically and turned her head away.

Luke untied the laces on the blue sneaker but, as he tried to ease the foot out of it, she gasped in pain, beads of sweat rolling down her face.

'Please. Just pull!'

He obliged, but as the foot came free the girl passed out cold again. With a savage curse he yanked his phone out of his back pocket. 'Spiro, the woman's had an accident. She's unconscious. The clinic will be shut at this hour so I'll have to bring her up to the house.' He cut off Spiro's exclamation. 'Find Dr Riga, please. Tell him it's urgent.'

Luke decided against trying to revive the girl. Better she stayed out of it while he manhandled her. Cursing because she was virtually naked except for scraps of pink fabric, he found a towel nearby and shook it free of sand to drape over the girl. He searched in a backpack lying at the foot of the rock, his lip curling as he found a notebook and pencils. But otherwise there was only a small purse with some currency, and a paperback novel in English. No identity. He hooked his arms into the straps but, as he bent to pick her up, her eyes flew open, wild with fear again.

'You are perfectly safe,' he snapped impatiently. 'I shall carry you to my boat.'

Luke was as careful as possible as he carried his burden across the narrow beach, but she was unconscious again by the time he deposited her in the well of the boat. In a black mood, he cast off and set off across the water on the short trip back to moor the boat at the marina, thankful, not for the first time, that his berth was well away from the tavernas. He secured the boat, then, praying she hadn't fractured her skull, Luke picked up his unconscious passenger who, though slender, was a dead weight. He braced himself, stepped up onto the quay and buckled her in the passenger seat of the Cherokee. Annoyed because he was breathing hard, he tucked the towel around her, shrugged off the backpack and drove back to the villa.

Spiro and Eleni hurried out to meet him, followed by Milos, the gardener, all of them exclaiming volubly over his unconscious passenger.

'My apologies, *kyrie*,' said Milos remorsefully. 'My mother needed me. What happened to the lady?'

'She fell on the rocks,' Luke growled, jumping out.

'Dr Riga is out on a call,' reported Spiro, looking worried.

Luke swallowed a curse. 'Will he be long?'

'Alex Nicolaides is home, *kyrie*. I saw him this morning. I could go down and fetch him,' Milos suggested.

Luke nodded grimly as he checked the girl's pulse. 'Get him here as fast as you can, please.'

'The poor young lady!' Eleni bent to mop the blood from the unconscious girl's temple as Milos rushed off. 'She has hurt her pretty face.'

'Let me help carry her upstairs,' offered Spiro, but Luke shook his head.

'I can manage. But I need you with me, please, Eleni.' As he released the safety belt the girl came round and struggled to sit upright, shrinking away from him in such terror that Luke's patience suddenly ran out.

'You are not in danger,' he snapped. 'I have brought you to my house.'

'No, really—I must get back to my cottage,' Isobel protested, horrified. Before he could stop her, she slid from the car, then gasped in agony as she put her weight on her injured ankle.

With a face like thunder, Luke scooped her up, ignoring Eleni's protests when the towel was left behind. He strode up the curving staircase to a large airy bedroom and deposited his unwilling burden in a chair. 'I will leave you with my housekeeper,' he panted and stalked out of the room.

The woman smiled sympathetically. 'I am Eleni. I speak a little English, but not good.' She took the girl's arm to help her over to the inviting white bed, but Isobel shook her head, a move she deeply regretted when the pain struck so hard the room swam before her eyes.

'Sick,' she gasped, clapping her hand to her mouth, and Eleni acted like lightning to help her hop into the adjoining bathroom. After a painful, humiliating episode, Isobel gasped her thanks and eventually gave in to Eleni's insistence that she remove the bikini, which had suffered badly during the day's various adventures. By this time totally beyond embarrassment, Isobel submitted to Eleni's ministrations as the woman helped her sponge her face and hot, aching body, then wrapped her in a white towelling robe.

'Thank—you—so—much,' said Isobel, teeth chattering in reaction as the woman helped her lie down against banked snowy pillows on the bed.

Eleni picked up the bikini. 'I wash this. You rest,' she said firmly and went out, closing the door behind her.

The session in the bathroom had rocketed Isobel's headache to hammer-blow dimensions, which almost blotted out the pain of her ankle but only accentuated her raging thirst as she tried to make sense of her accident. She remembered some idiot on a Jet Ski coming straight at the beach from the sea, then hitting her head and nothing else until she opened her eyes on the angry, handsome face of a stranger and assumed he was the culprit. Which had infuriated him. She tensed as the door opened and her hostile rescuer approached the bed.

'How do you feel?' he asked curtly.

'Not too well.' She swallowed. 'I'm so sorry to be a nuisance, but could I possibly have some water?'

Cursing silently for not thinking of it first, Luke nodded stiffly. 'Of course.'

Isobel watched him as he strode out of the room. He was tall, with a fabulous physique, and in a better mood would be very good-looking. Not that she was concerned with his hostility, or with anything else other than how in the world she was going to get herself out of here—wherever 'here' was—and get back to the little cottage she'd paid good money for. And one day of her holiday was already ruined. Tears leaked out of her eyes at the thought, but she knuckled them away, impatient with self-pity as her host returned with her backpack, followed by Eleni with a tray. The woman poured water into a glass and handed it to Isobel, then, at a look from her employer, went from the room, leaving the door wide open.

'Eleni has looked after my family for years,' he stated.

Desperate to gulp the water down, Isobel forced herself to sip cautiously. 'She's very kind.'

'I am not?'

'Of course.' Her face grew even hotter. 'I'm extremely grateful to you. And very embarrassed for causing so much trouble.'

Luke shrugged negligently. 'Tell me your name.'

'Isobel James.' She drank the rest of the water and held the cold glass to her cheek, eyeing him questioningly. 'And you are?'

He laughed scornfully. 'You do not know?'

She stiffened. 'I'm afraid not. I only arrived on the island yesterday.'

His dark eyes narrowed to a cynical glitter. 'So why were you on my beach? You paid someone to take you there by boat?'

Isobel's knuckles clenched on the glass. 'No. I went down the path nearest the cottage to the beach adjoining yours. But by mid-morning it was crowded, so when I spotted the gap in the rocks I went to explore.'

'That way is blocked!'

'Not quite. I managed to squeeze through.'

'You were so determined to invade my privacy?' His eyes flamed with distaste, which touched Isobel on the raw.

'Certainly not,' she snapped. 'I had no idea it was a private beach, nor who it belonged to. I apologise—*humbly*—for trespassing. And now, if you'll be kind enough to call a taxi, I'll get dressed and leave.'

He raised a cynical eyebrow. 'And how do you propose to walk?'

'I'll manage,' she snapped, praying she was right.

Eleni knocked at the open door and ushered in a familiar figure armed with a medical bag. The two men embraced each other and exchanged greetings before Alex Nicolaides moved to the bed, his eyes wide in consternation as he recognised his patient. 'Miss James! What happened?' He turned to her glowering rescuer, obviously asking him the same question in his own language.

'The lady,' Luke informed him in very deliberate English, 'was trespassing on my private beach when she suffered a fall. She was unconscious when I found her. Thank you for coming, Doctor. Please examine her injuries and tell me what must be done for her.'

'I need Eleni to stay, please,' said Isobel urgently.

Luke motioned the woman to the bed, but stayed at the foot of it, obviously determined to monitor the proceedings.

Eleni patted Isobel's hand comfortingly as Alex bent over her.

'This is very bad luck for you, Miss James,' he said gently.

His sympathy was so genuine tears welled in Isobel's eyes, burning as they trickled down her flushed cheeks. Eleni produced tissues to dry the patient's face so Alex could examine the wound, then he shone a torch in her eyes, held up a finger and told her to follow it with each eye in turn.

'You have vomited?'

'Yes.'

'Does your head hurt very badly?'

'Yes.'

'Examine her foot; she hurt that, also,' Luke said, sounding bored.

Alex frowned as he eyed the swollen ankle. 'It is necessary to examine for fracture,' he told Isobel. 'I will be quick.'

'Careful,' warned Luke. 'She faints a lot.'

A lot? Until today, she'd never fainted before in her life!

Isobel clenched her teeth, determined not to faint again as Alex probed gently, though at one point it was a near thing.

'The ankle is badly sprained only, not broken, Miss James,' Alex assured her. 'I will apply temporary bandage, then report to Dr Riga, who will take X-rays to confirm. I will also put a dressing on your face, and give you mild painkillers. Take with much fluid.'

'Thank you.' She tried to relax as he strapped her ankle. 'Did you come here in a car, Doctor?'

He looked up in surprise. 'No, on back of Milos's motor-bike. Why?'

'I was hoping for a lift back to the cottage,' she said, disappointed, and eyed him in appeal. 'Would you be kind enough to arrange a taxi for me?'

Alex shot a startled look at Luke, who showed his teeth in a cold smile.

'Miss James may stay here as long as she wishes.'

Not one second longer, if she could help it. 'How kind,' said Isobel frostily. 'But I wouldn't dream of inconveniencing you. So will you sort out a taxi for me, Doctor?'

Alex looked so uncomfortable Luke took pity on him.

'I will drive you myself, Miss James,' he said impatiently. 'But only when you can manage alone. Demonstrate this for us.'

Isobel summoned every scrap of willpower she possessed to sit up straight. She paused for breath, swivelled round until she could put her good foot on the floor and then took the hand Eleni held out to help her as she struggled to stand. 'You see?' she said through her teeth. 'If you gentlemen will kindly leave, I'll get dressed.'

'Miss James, this is not a good idea,' said Alex, plainly expecting her to collapse in a heap at any second.

'I must try. The cottage is all on one floor. I have food there, so if Mr—'

She glanced at her host. 'I'm afraid I don't know your name.'

'No?' He raised an eyebrow in scornful disbelief. 'I am Lukas Andreadis.'

'How do you do?' She turned to Alex. 'If Mr Andreadis will drive me, I'll be just fine.' She swallowed hard on rising nausea and wavered slightly, her hand tightening on Eleni's.

Luke shook his head. 'I will drive you when you *are* fine, Miss James, but that is most obviously not today. Put her back, Eleni.'

'That is best, Luke,' said Alex, relieved.

Isobel gave up. She let Eleni make her comfortable, then turned her face into the pillows in despair. Her longed-for odyssey had come to a grinding halt before it had even started. She ignored the hushed interchange in their own tongue between the men, wishing they'd just go away and leave her to wallow alone in her misery.

'Miss James,' said Alex, coming back to the bed.

Isobel opened her eyes. 'Yes?'

'If you allow me to have your keys, I will take my sister to your house to pack for you.'

'How kind,' she said unsteadily. 'The keys are in my backpack.'

'I am most happy to do this, but it was Luke's idea,' he added.

She turned unsmiling eyes on her host. 'Then thank you, too, Mr Andreadis.'

'Here in Greece we believe in helping travellers,' he informed her indifferently.

'Unless they invade your beach.'

'True.' He unbent enough to smile faintly. 'Come, then, Alex. I will drive you.'

Eleni closed the door behind them, poured iced fruit juice

into a glass and gave Isobel two of the tablets. 'Drink, *kyria*,' she said firmly.

Isobel obediently swallowed the painkillers and drank some of the juice. '*Efcharisto*, Eleni.' She managed a smile. 'But please call me Isobel.'

Eleni repeated the name shyly, put the glass on the table, then opened the carton of yoghurt.

Isobel eyed it in alarm. 'I'm so sorry, but I really can't eat anything right now.'

'*Ochee*, not for eating. For your face. It is burning, *ne*?'

'Oh, yes,' sighed Isobel, and submitted to an unexpected beauty treatment. Eleni smoothed the blessedly cool, creamy yoghurt over her face, left it there until it warmed up, then gently cleaned it off with tissues.

'I will do it more later,' she promised, 'but now you sleep, Isobel.' She smiled and went from the room, leaving the door ajar.

Eventually the pills took enough edge off her aches and pains to let Isobel take interest in her surroundings. Filmy white curtains stirred at glass doors which led on to a balcony, and the room itself was furnished with the type of elegant simplicity that cost the earth. She groaned in sudden despair. She'd come all this way to Chyros to regain her normal perspective on life, yet one day into her holiday and here she was, stranded in a wealthy—and hugely unfriendly—stranger's house, with no way of escaping until she was more mobile. But why had the man been so sure she'd known who he was? And felt so ticked off about it, too. Perhaps he was some kind of celebrity here in Greece. Her mouth twisted. He needn't worry where she was concerned. He was good-looking enough in a forceful kind of way, but his personality was so horribly overbearing it cancelled out any attraction he might have had for her as a man...

When Isobel opened her eyes again they widened when she found another stranger looking down at her.

'Dr Riga, Isobel,' said Eleni, hurrying to help her to sit up.

The large, bespectacled man gave her a reassuring smile. '*Kalispera*. How do you feel?' he asked in heavily accented English, and took her pulse.

'Not too well,' she admitted.

He nodded, his eyes so sympathetic her own filled with tears again.

'I'm so sorry, Doctor,' she said huskily, and took the tissue Eleni had ready.

'You suffer much pain; you are also in shock and alone in a strange country, Miss James. Tears are natural,' he assured her. 'I must take X-ray at my clinic. Eleni will help you dress.' He smiled reassuringly and went from the room.

'Eleni,' said Isobel urgently, 'will you help me wash again? Did Mr Andreadis bring my clothes?'

The woman nodded and helped Isobel out of the bed, supporting her as she hopped awkwardly to the bathroom. 'I used iron,' she said severely. 'Alyssa Nicolaides packed too quick.'

'You're an angel, thank you, Eleni.' Isobel tried to hurry. 'I mustn't keep the doctor waiting.'

Eleni shook her head. 'He is gone. *Kyrie* Luke will drive you. Not rush,' she warned.

After the hurried bathroom session Isobel felt relatively presentable in a white denim skirt and blue T-shirt, though the effect was marred by wearing only one sandal. Otherwise she felt horribly queasy still, and her head was pounding like a war drum. Eleni helped her to the stool in front of the dressing table, anointed her face with more yoghurt, then wiped it away and handed Isobel her zippered travel pack. Resigned to see faint bruising under her eye, Isobel used a comb gingerly, decided against lip gloss and smiled wanly at Eleni.

'I'm ready.'

The woman nodded. 'I tell him.'

Isobel would have given a lot to walk downstairs on her own two feet when Luke Andreadis appeared in the doorway in a crisp white shirt and jeans which were obviously custom made by their fit.

'How do you feel now?' he asked, his eyes on the bright hair curling loosely on her shoulders.

'Cleaner.'

'But you are still in pain.'

'Yes.'

He picked her up with exaggerated care. 'I will strive not to cause you more.'

'Likewise, Mr Andreadis,' she returned, holding herself rigid, face averted, as he carried her from the room.

He frowned. 'Likewise?'

'Carrying me around can't be doing your back much good.'

He laughed sardonically as he descended the curving staircase into a marble-floored hall with an alcove containing a striking half-size statue of Perseus brandishing the severed head of the gorgon Medusa. 'I will survive. You are not heavy.'

'As soon as humanly possible, I'll get back to the cottage.'

'When Dr Riga says you are fit to do so,' he said dismissively and carried her through a large plant-filled conservatory to put her in the passenger seat of the Cherokee Jeep parked at the back of the villa. Which, now she had attention to spare for it, Isobel could see was a dream of a house.

'You have a beautiful home,' she said politely as Luke got in beside her.

'*Efcharisto*. I bought it years ago, and altered it to suit my taste. I look on it—and the beach that came with it—as my private retreat.'

'Is that why you were so furious when you found me down there?'

He lifted a shoulder. 'Trespassers are a common occurrence.'

She clenched her teeth. 'Once again, I apologise.'

It was no surprise to find that Luke Andreadis drove with panache. They swerved at speed round one dizzying bend after another on the tortuous descent until at last Isobel had to beg him to stop.

Luke came to a screaming halt, raced round the Jeep and hauled her out, then, to her hideous embarrassment, supported her as she retched miserably over a clump of bushes at the roadside.

'Can you continue now?' he demanded as she straightened.

'Yes,' she gasped, sending up a prayer that she was right.

He put her back in the Jeep and handed her bag over. 'I will drive slowly the rest of the way,' he said stiffly.

'Thank you,' she managed, the pain in her head now so unbearable again she could hardly speak.

The doctor hurried out of the modern clinic building as they arrived, his face anxious.

'You are late. I was worried.'

'We had to stop on the way because Miss James was sick,' Luke informed him. 'I am so used to the road I drove too fast.'

'Ah, poor child. Bring her in, Lukas. My radiologist is waiting, and also Nurse Pappas with a wheelchair.'

Luke lifted Isobel out of the car to transfer her to the wheelchair, his mouth tightening as he felt her shrink from him. 'You will obviously prefer this.'

You bet, thought Isobel, as the friendly nurse wheeled her

away. Later, after X-rays and a trying episode while her wound was thoroughly cleaned and dressed again, she was given painkillers and water, then wheeled back to the reception area.

'There is no fracture to the skull or the ankle, but you are suffering from mild concussion,' Dr Riga reported and smiled encouragingly at Isobel. 'You need light nourishment and much rest. I will give you more medication for the headache, but take no more until bedtime. And Nurse Pappas has a crutch for you.'

'Thank you,' said Isobel gratefully, smiling at both of them.

'Are you ready?' Luke tossed the crutch in the back of the Jeep, then installed Isobel in the passenger seat. His face was so grim as he took the wheel; the drive back to the villa was accomplished in silence so tense until Isobel felt obliged, at last, to break it.

'I'm very grateful for all your help, Mr Andreadis,' she said formally. 'Would you give me Dr Riga's bill, please?'

'I have settled it,' he said dismissively.

'Then I will pay you,' she persisted.

Luke Andreadis, accustomed to women who expected him to foot bills far more expensive than Dr Riga's, shot her a scathing look. 'I require no money from you, Miss James.'

Isobel had no energy to argue, even though the mere thought of owing this man anything at all acted like fire on her skin—which was hot enough already.

Once back at his house, Luke lifted Isobel out, then handed her the crutch. 'Welcome back to the Villa Medusa,' he said formally. 'You can manage with this?'

'Yes, thank you.' Even if it killed her. But, by the time they made it through the conservatory, Isobel felt too exhausted to protest when Luke handed Spiro the crutch and picked her up to carry her upstairs.

CHAPTER TWO

ELENI and Spiro hurried behind, listening closely as Luke reported in their own language on Dr Riga's treatment.

'Eleni asked when you last ate,' he reported, letting Isobel down in the armchair.

'This morning on your beach,' she gasped. No point in mentioning that grapes had been the only thing on the menu. Nor that she'd parted with them and everything else in her system in the guest bathroom, with an encore on the way down to the clinic.

'I bring food to you very soon, Isobel,' promised Eleni.

Relieved to have her catering arrangements decided for her, Isobel smiled wearily. '*Efcharisto*, Eleni. But I'm not at all hungry.'

Luke took the crutch from Spiro and propped it against Isobel's chair. 'You have everything you need?'

Heartily sick of being heaved around by a man who made it so plain it was a tiresome chore, Isobel made no attempt at a polite smile. 'Yes. Thank you. I shan't trouble you again.'

Luke's smile set her teeth on edge. 'You were trouble from the moment I first saw you, on my flight over the beach.'

'Flight?'

'In my helicopter. It is my habit to scan the beach as I come in to land.'

'To scope out trespassers!' She looked him in the eye—or as well as she could with one of her own half closed. 'At the risk of boring you, I apologise once again for my intrusion, Mr Andreadis.' Her mouth twisted. 'Lord knows, I suffered such swift retribution I'll never do it again.'

'Even though you failed in your aim?'

Isobel frowned, her thought processes fighting a losing battle with her headache. 'I don't understand.'

Luke eyed the motionless Spiro, who obviously intended standing his ground until his employer was ready to leave. 'With your permission, Miss James,' continued Luke, 'I will return after you have eaten. I wish to talk to you.'

Isobel inclined her sore head gingerly. As if she could say no!

Alone, she sagged for a moment in relief, then pulled herself together and tried putting her crutch through its paces. To her intense satisfaction she found that, headache and sprained ankle or not, she was now mobile, if not agile. Hallelujah! After the talk with the hostile Mr Andreadis, a lift back to the cottage was all the help she would need from him.

When Eleni came in, followed by Spiro with a tray, Isobel smiled persuasively and pointed to the balcony doors. 'Could I eat out there, please?'

'It is dark,' said the woman, astonished.

'Not with the stars and the light from the lamps in here.'

'Whatever you wish, *kyria*,' said Spiro, and took the tray out to the small table on the balcony. He rearranged the chairs, opened the other door to make it easier for her and bowed to her, smiling.

'*Efcharisto*, Spiro,' said Isobel gratefully and limped out onto the balcony to sit at the table, smiling in such triumph at Eleni as she parked the crutch that the woman laughed and patted her shoulder.

'You are better. Good, good. Now, eat.' She took a silver cover from an inviting omelette and left Isobel to her solitary meal.

To her surprise, Isobel's taste buds sprang to life with the first mouthful. Once it seemed her stomach meant to behave, she ate all the omelette and some of the salad and bread that came with it, finding that eating alone, with only the stars for company, did wonders for her appetite. Isobel drank some water and then sat back to gaze out over the garden, her eyes fixed in longing on the floodlit pool. She'd love a swim in it before she went back to her cottage. But fond hope of that with Mr Congeniality on the premises.

A knock on the bedroom door brought her out of her reverie. She picked up the crutch and went slowly into the room, smiling at Eleni. 'It was a lovely supper. I've taken some pills and I feel much better now.'

'Good, good,' said the woman, beaming. 'I bring more yoghurt for face. Use before bed. I help you to bathroom now?'

'No, thank you. I can manage myself.'

The woman frowned. 'Then I come back later when time to sleep.'

'All right, Eleni,' sighed Isobel, knowing when she was beaten. 'Before you go, could you put the big chair near the veranda doors? *Efcharisto poli.*'

Isobel eyed her reflection critically in the large bathroom mirror. Her eye was ringed with interesting shades of plum, but at least it was now almost open again, and her sunburn had toned down, thanks to Eleni's yoghurt. Pleased with her new mobility, Isobel limped back into the room to sit in the big, comfortable chair, content just to look out into the night while she waited for her visitor.

'Come in,' she called later, in answer to the expected knock.

Luke strolled in, his eyes on her face. '*Kalispera*. You look better. Eleni tells me you ate most of your supper.'

'Yes. It was delicious.' Isobel sat still and tense, wondering what he wanted to talk about.

'May I sit down?'

'Of course.'

Luke drew the dressing table stool nearer Isobel and stood by it for a moment. 'Shall I fetch your notebook? Since you suffered so much to achieve it, I have decided to grant your interview.'

Isobel stared at him blankly. 'Interview?'

'I collected your belongings on the beach,' he informed her. 'There was a notebook, also several pencils in your bag. Do you deny that you are a journalist, Miss James?'

Isobel took in a deep calming breath, then took the pad from the backpack on the floor beside her and handed it over. 'Look for yourself.'

Luke's mouth tightened as he turned over pages of drawings. 'What are these?'

'I would have thought that's obvious, Mr Andreadis. I drew the boats from the veranda of the cottage when I first arrived, and the other sketch this morning on the beach next to yours. Ideally, I would have used watercolour, but I had no way of getting the materials down such a steep path.' Isobel looked at him coldly. 'Other people take holiday snaps. I make sketches.'

'Which,' he said slowly, leafing through them again, 'are most accomplished.'

'Thank you.'

Luke ran a hand through his thick curls, then looked up, surveying her in silence for so long that Isobel grew restive. 'It is now I who must make apology,' he said at last, as though the words were drawn out of him with pincers.

'Accepted.' She eyed him curiously. 'You dislike journalists and guard your privacy very fiercely, Mr Andreadis, so
are you some kind of celebrity here in Greece?'

He shook his head. 'No, just a successful businessman,
Miss James. I am in shipping, but also much in the news
lately, due to a successful takeover of a private airline.' His
mouth turned down. 'And I have no wife. This also attracts
interest from the press.'

'About whether you're gay?' she said, secretly delighted
by the look of outrage on his face.

'*Ochee*! I may lack a wife, but it is common knowledge
that I enjoy the company of women. Did *you* think I was
gay?' he demanded.

'Not easy to tell on such brief acquaintance.'

His eyes narrowed to a glitter, which put her on the alert.
'Even though we have been in enforced physical contact from
the first moment of our meeting?'

Isobel's face heated. 'I wasn't conscious for most of it.
And, now that I am, no further contact is necessary. Not,' she
added hastily, 'that I'm ungrateful for your help.'

He shrugged. 'I had no choice but to give it, Miss James.'

She eyed him in disdain. 'You made that very clear—but
I'm grateful just the same.'

His eyes softened. 'It has been a bad start to your holiday.'

'It has indeed.' She pushed her hair away from her throbbing forehead. 'So, if you can spare the time to drive me to
my cottage tomorrow to get on with it, I'd be very grateful,
Mr Andreadis.'

'You cannot manage alone there yet,' he said dismissively.

'I most certainly can. There is absolutely no difference
between getting myself around this room and doing the same
at the cottage.'

'And how will you feed yourself?'

She'd been prepared for that. 'If Eleni will buy food for me before I go, I'll manage very well until I can walk properly again. My ankle feels better already,' she lied. 'In a day or so I'll be back to normal.'

He eyed her in silence for a moment. 'Before you make your escape from the Villa Medusa, please indulge my curiosity. Tell me something about yourself. From your drawings, your interest obviously lies in art, Miss James.'

'Yes. I have a Fine Art Degree.'

'You teach?'

'No. I manage an art gallery and live in the flat over it as part of a deal which includes putting my work on sale at the gallery, as well as the paintings I sell privately.'

'You live near your family?'

Isobel looked down at the hands she'd folded in her lap. 'No. My wonderful grandparents brought me up, but they're dead now.'

Luke leaned forward slightly. 'And your parents?'

'I never knew them. They were killed in a motorway pile-up in fog when I was a baby.'

'That is a sad story,' he said sombrely. 'But you were fortunate to have grandparents who cared for you.'

'True. They were the only parents I ever knew, and I couldn't have wished for better. But, though I'm short on family, I'm blessed with very good friends,' said Isobel, trying to ignore her headache. 'In the past my holidays were spent with one of them but, since her marriage a couple of years ago, I travel alone.'

Luke got up. 'Have you informed this friend of your accident?'

'I saw no point in worrying her. I'll be fine in a day or two.'

'But you are not fine now. Your headache is bad again, yes?'

'Afraid so,' she admitted.

He looked down at her, frowning. 'I shall send Eleni to help you to bed.' He held up a peremptory hand. 'Yes, I know you can manage without her, but she insisted. Is there anything you would like her to bring you?'

Isobel smiled hopefully. 'I would really love some tea.'

'Of course. You shall have it immediately. *Kalmychta*— goodnight, Miss James.'

'Goodnight, Mr Andreadis.'

Isobel was very thoughtful after he'd gone, wondering why he'd asked so many questions. It made her doubly wary of Lukas Andreadis, mainly because her current opinion of his sex was at an all-time low. But, looked at objectively, from an artistic point of view he was a formidable specimen, with the physique and sculpted features of the Greek statues she'd studied in college. Though more like the Renaissance muscular versions than the androgynous Apollo Belvedere of Ancient Greece. Similar curls, maybe, but Luke Andreadis was very obviously all male, his impressive build a definite plus when it came to carrying her about. His one concession to vanity seemed to be the hair he grew long enough to brush his collar. But she would have expected those curls of his to be black, like his eyes. Instead, they were bronze with lighter streaks, courtesy of the sun. Her mouth tightened. Good-looking he might be, but when she'd first seen him, down on his precious private beach, he'd been so menacing he'd frightened her to death.

Isobel took more painkillers with the tea Eleni brought her, then submitted to her yoghurt beauty treatment and let the kind little woman help her to bed. Isobel thanked Eleni warmly, wished her goodnight, and then settled down against banked pillows and, though fully expecting to lie awake for hours with her aches and pains for company, eventually drifted off into healing, dreamless sleep.

CHAPTER THREE

LUKE ANDREADIS asked Eleni to take tea up to their guest, then went to his room, but felt too restless for sleep. He made for his balcony with a glass of brandy and leaned against the rail, breathing in the heady nocturnal scents of the garden. After the punishing campaign of the past few weeks he felt anti-climactic, already missing the adrenaline rush of corporate battle. His mouth curled in grim triumph as he relived the victory over Melina Andreadis. She must be incandescent with fury now she no longer controlled the airline acquired by the husband who had once given it to his demanding second wife as if it were a toy to play with. But now, Luke thought triumphantly, she had been rendered powerless. Her ties with the airline had been severed without mercy by the grandson Theo Andreadis refused to acknowledge.

Luke raised his glass to the stars in exultation at the memory of Melina's fury, of her ageing face, scarlet and suffused with rage. It had been worth every minute of his years of hard, unending work just to see the harpy's face when the vote went against her. Whoever said revenge was a dish best served cold was right on target. His long fight to wreak revenge on Melina had left little room in his life for personal relationships. But this mattered very little to him now he had finally exacted his revenge. His only sorrow was that his mother had not lived to share in his triumph. His face set in implacable lines. That she was not was another sin to lay at his grandfather's door. Theo Andreadis had brought up his motherless daughter so strictly her eventual rebellion had been inevitable. The discovery that she was pregnant had enraged her father so much he'd thrown her out on the street. The desperate girl had fled from Athens to take refuge with her old nurse on Chyros, where Olympia Andreadis, daughter of one of the richest men in Greece, had supported herself by working in the kitchen of the taverna owned by Basil Nicolaides, father of the present owner, Nikos.

Luke's eyes darkened at the thought of his frail, pretty mother, who had escaped from her home in Athens with only the jewels inherited from her mother. These had provided savings hoarded zealously for her child as he grew into a clever, determined boy who soon outstripped his peers academically at school. Young Lukas absorbed knowledge like a sponge and, with the help of a young, enthusiastic teacher early on, became fluent in English, which added to his prowess in all the other subjects on the school curriculum. Fuelled by determination to help his mother, he did odd jobs after school at the taverna to earn money, and at weekends, much to Olympia's disapproval, went out with the local fishermen for the same purpose. He would have done anything to protect his mother from the blandishments of Costas Petrides, the wealthiest man on the island. Costas had been so eager to marry the exquisite, cultured Olympia he had even professed willingness to take her illegitimate son as part of the deal. But she had politely and relentlessly refused, secure in the protection of Spiro, son of her old nurse, and the support of Basil Nicolaides and his son Nikos, who jointly managed the taverna. But Luke well knew that to this day Costas blamed Olympia's son for her refusal of such a good catch for a husband.

Luke grew up in a home where there was much love, but very little money. As he grew to adulthood he became consumed with the desire to keep his mother in luxury for the rest of her days, to repay Spiro and the Nikolaides family for their kindness, and eventually to wreak merciless revenge on those responsible for his mother's situation, with Melina Andreadis at the top of his hit list.

And he had succeeded. He had rendered Melina powerless with the best weapon of all, the loss of backing from her own board. He smiled with grim satisfaction at the memory of her raging, impotent fury as the vote went against her. For a moment it had seemed likely she would attack him with her own red-taloned fingers as the truth struck home that she was powerless to fight against fate when the airline was torn from her grasp. And now Lukas Andreadis was the power behind Air Chyros, the new name he'd given his grandfather's airline. In the future, instead of making money with as many cheap flights as possible under the grasping Melina's aegis, it would be run with the emphasis on safety, reliability and luxury, the key elements Air Chyros would be offering once the new planes were in operation.

Luke drank down the last of his brandy and turned back into his room, wincing as the odd muscle protested. He smiled a little. He prided himself on his fitness, which he swam daily to maintain, but it wasn't every day he was required to rescue a damsel in distress. A very appealing damsel, he admitted, though tumbling blonde curls and big blue eyes were not female assets which normally appealed to him. He liked his women dark, with fiery temperaments and ample curves—he laughed shortly, giving thanks to the gods that he hadn't been obliged to carry a woman of that description about, or he might have had more than just a sore muscle or two to complain about. But, even though Miss Isobel James looked the picture of innocence, he still harboured doubts about her reasons for her presence on his beach this morning. Yet her stoicism and independence—and the feel of her slender body in his arms—appealed strongly to him. While she, very obviously, was finding it difficult to be grateful to a man she regarded with suspicion, even dislike. A new experience for him where women were concerned. He smiled slowly. Now he was here for a few days it would be diverting to see how quickly he could break down the barrier she'd erected against him. He must think up ways of keeping her here until he achieved his usual success. His mouth twisted in self-derision as he realised that a great part of the lady's attraction was her immunity to his own—a challenge impossible to resist.

Blissfully unaware of her host's plans for her immediate future, Isobel woke early again next morning and for a moment gazed blankly round the unfamiliar room until a glance at the crutch leaning against the foot of the bed brought the events of the previous day rushing back. She lay quiet for a while as she reviewed them, amazed that she'd survived the night without one of the nightmares afflicting her lately. Perhaps she was cured of them at last. She was so comfortable she was reluctant to move, but at last she had no choice. With a sigh Isobel sat up, carefully manoeuvred herself to the edge of the bed, reached for the crutch and put her good foot to the floor. Twenty minutes later she was sitting by the open veranda doors, hair combed, teeth brushed, face clean and painkillers washed down with fruit juice. And, though both ankle and head were still making their presence felt, the discomfort was bearable enough to confirm that once she transferred to the cottage she would be able to manage perfectly well on her own.

She looked up with a smile as Eleni appeared with a breakfast tray. 'Good morning.'

The little woman returned the smile shyly. '*Kalimera*. How you feel today, Isobel?'

'Much better,' Isobel assured her. 'Thank you, Eleni. You're a star.'

Eleni carried the tray out on to the veranda, leaving the doors open wide for Isobel. 'Eat well,' she commanded, and left Isobel to the pleasure of breakfast in the fresh air of a Chyros morning.

Thankful to find her nausea gone, Isobel ate one of the sweet rolls and finished off the tea, looking down in longing through the balcony rails at the pool. She sucked in a sudden breath. A bronzed body had appeared in the water, cutting through it like some exotic sea creature as Lukas swam laps of his pool at a speed that tired Isobel to watch. At last he heaved himself out of the water to stand with arms outstretched and face upturned to the sun for a minute or two before he wrapped his spectacular body in a towelling robe.

Isobel let out the breath she hadn't even known she was holding, wondering how to get herself off the balcony without attracting his attention. But before she could move he turned, gave her a mocking bow and strolled into the house.

Face flaming, Isobel did her Long John Silver act back into the bedroom to strip off her dressing gown. Time she moved out. She collected some clothes and a polythene bag used to pack shoes, and then went into the bathroom for a sponge down. It was a messy, unsatisfactory process, but she managed it without wetting the bandage on her ankle, and felt absurdly pleased with herself when it was over. She slapped on some body lotion, struggled into her underwear, then pulled on a favourite comfortable yellow T-shirt dress and, with the help of the crutch, made it back into the bedroom just as Eleni hurried in.

'I came to help,' said the woman reproachfully.

Isobel smiled in apology. 'I had to see if I could manage on my own. I really must leave today and go back to the cottage. I'm afraid I used rather a lot of towels.'

The woman shrugged this off as unimportant, and went into the bathroom to collect them. 'You sit still now. I bring coffee,' she said firmly, and took the damp bundle away.

Isobel did her sitting still on the balcony, determined not to remain in the vicinity of Lukas Andreadis a moment longer than necessary. When Eleni came back with the coffee she would request a visit from the master of the house, preferably when he was fully clothed, and ask him for a lift down to the cottage. After that she need never see him again. Which would be good because she found his presence disturbing. For one thing, he was a man, and for another she was sure he still believed she'd been up to no good when she invaded his precious beach. While all she wanted from him was a lift back to the cottage so she could enjoy the rest of her holiday alone, in the peace she'd come all this way to find.

When she called in answer to a knock on the bedroom door she heard the slight rattling of a tray and sniffed the enticing scent of freshly made coffee. But, instead of Eleni, it was Luke Andreadis, casual in jeans and T-shirt, who came out onto the veranda to put a tray down on the table.

'*Kalimera*,' he greeted her. 'May I join you?'

'Of course,' she said, hiding her dismay. 'Good morning.'

'How are you today?'

'Much better.'

'Eleni tells me you did not wait for her to help you dress,' he said casually.

'I had to try to manage on my own.'

Luke handed her a cup of coffee, then pulled a chair up to the table. 'I trust,' he said, eyeing her ankle, 'that your bandage is still dry?'

'I wrapped my foot in a plastic bag.' She smiled politely. 'I'm self-sufficient now. So if you'd be kind enough to drive me down to the cottage this morning I'll leave you in peace.'

He shook his damp head. 'Not this morning.'

Isobel's heart sank. 'This afternoon, then?'

'Before you can stay there alone, food must be bought for you.'

'I'll give you money for Eleni,' she said promptly.

'Also,' he went on, brushing that aside, 'I must inspect the place for myself first, to check its suitability for your injury.'

Her chin lifted. 'There's absolutely no need for you to trouble yourself, Mr Andreadis,' she said flatly. 'If I can manage here, I can manage there.'

He raised an eyebrow. 'Also cook for yourself?'

'With a supply of salad vegetables, and bread and cheese, I shan't need to cook for myself for a day or two. And by then I'll be good on both feet,' she assured him, resenting his tone.

'If you will give me your key I shall go down to the cottage soon,' said Luke. 'And then we shall see.'

Isobel sighed, frustrated. 'If you must. Though I thought you'd be only too pleased to get rid of me.'

His smile set off alarm bells in her head. 'As I told you, Miss James, we revere the traveller here in Greece.'

'You were anything but reverent when you found this one on your beach!'

'Only because I misunderstood the reason for your presence.' And strongly doubted her story of the Jet Ski. His eyes darkened. 'It is by no means unusual for journalists of both sexes to invade my beach, nor for young women to arrange to be stranded there.'

'In the hope that you'll come to the rescue?'

'Their hopes are usually higher—or lower—than that,' he said, his mouth twisting in distaste. 'I do not,' he added sardonically, 'delude myself that they are attracted to me in person. Only to my money.'

'And the power you used to amass it. Isn't power supposed to be the ultimate aphrodisiac?' Isobel smiled politely. 'You Greeks have a word for everything.'

He inclined his head. 'The rest of the world owes much to us.'

'What happens to trespassers when you're not here?'

'Milos deals with them. He is ex-army, and officially works as my gardener. But his main function is security. He had time off yesterday; otherwise you would have been removed before I arrived.'

'Which would have saved a lot of trouble.' One way and another.

Luke gave her the unsettling smile again. 'But it would also have deprived me of the pleasure of meeting you.'

Isobel dismissed that with a shrug. 'You speak very good English.'

'Thank you. I had a very good English teacher in school and, due to his influence, I studied for my MBA in London.' He got up. 'It is good you are not a journalist. I am not usually free with my personal details.'

'I shan't pass them on to anyone,' she assured him.

He looked surprised. 'They are not secrets. I was born here on Chyros. My background is known to everyone.'

'Even so, I don't speak Greek so I'm not likely to talk to anyone about you.'

'Not even to Alex Nicolaides? He speaks English.'

'He hardly knows me! Though he was very helpful,' she added.

'Which cannot surprise you.'

She raised an eyebrow in silent query.

'A look in the mirror will answer your question,' he informed her.

She sighed. Same old, same old. 'I seriously doubt that. I have a black eye, in case you haven't noticed, Mr Andreadis.'

'I could hardly help notice, but it is already fading and detracts very little from your looks, Miss James.'

'Thank you,' she said shortly, and bent to pick up her handbag. 'Here are the keys. Will you let me know your verdict as soon as possible?'

Luke took them, his eyes amused. 'You are so eager to leave my house?'

Her chin lifted. 'I really can't *trespass* on your hospitality any longer.'

'You throw the word at me like a missile!' He chuckled. 'I shall see you at lunch.'

Isobel scowled as he strolled from the room, feeling all at sea. Lukas Andreadis in friendly mode—if you could call it that—was deeply unnerving. Yet hearing something of his background had whetted her curiosity to know more. But Eleni was the only one she could ask, so there was no way she was going to find out any more unless he told her himself. And, since she was hopefully moving out today, and it wasn't a question she could ask anyway, that was unlikely. But she couldn't leave until Luke Andreadis drove her to the cottage, so she would do what she always did with time on her hands—and far too often when she should have been doing other things entirely.

Isobel established herself at the balcony rail, propped one of her larger pads against it and began to sketch the pool. In the bright morning light it shone like a blue jewel in its setting of palms, oleander and feathery pink tamarisk. And as usual her concentration was soon so intense that Eleni had to clap her hands loudly to gain her attention.

'Lunch, Isobel.'

Isobel closed the sketchbook hastily and turned to smile at Eleni. 'I hadn't realised it was so late.'

'You wash now,' said the woman. 'Food nearly ready. You need help?'

'No, I can manage, thank you.' Isobel spent a few minutes in the bathroom, then went back into the bedroom to find Luke standing outside on the landing.

'Eleni says you must come immediately or the food will spoil,' he informed her. 'I will carry you down.'

Isobel flushed, taken aback. 'I thought I was eating up here again.'

'While I thought you would enjoy lunch on the terrace. Even with the disadvantage of my company,' he added slyly.

Isobel eyed him irritably. If she'd had prior knowledge of the arrangement, out of sheer pride she might have gilded the lily a bit—or as much as she could in her present condition. The swelling on her face had gone down, the bruise was fading slightly below her eye, which she could now open fully, but it was still no pleasure to look in a mirror. 'You don't have to carry me. I can manage with the crutch.'

'That will take too long, and Eleni will be very annoyed if her food is kept waiting,' he informed her and, ignoring her involuntary recoil, picked her up. Isobel tensed, for the first time physically aware of Luke as a man. She felt enveloped in the warmth and scent of him, and wanted to beat him away with clenched fists.

'Eleni didn't warn me,' she said, voice stifled, as Luke carried her down the curving staircase to the hall.

'I told her not to.'

'Why?'

'You would have refused.'

'I hope my manners are better than that, Mr Andreadis!'

He took her through open glass doors to a pergola wreathed with greenery on the section of terrace overlooking the pool. He set her down at a table laid for lunch. 'I think that under the circumstances we can dispense with formality. I am Luke.'

Bad idea. 'I'm Isobel,' she said reluctantly.

'Much better,' he said, and sat opposite her. 'Will you have some wine?'

'In deference to my head, I think I'd better stick with water.'

'Ah, yes—excuse me for a moment.' He went back into the house and returned with a walking stick. 'Borrow this. When you no longer need the crutch you might find it useful.'

Isobel's eyes lit up, winning an arrested look from him. 'I will, indeed. Thank you.' She hooked the stick over the arm of her chair. 'Wonderful. Now I'm completely self-sufficient. What did you think of the cottage?'

He smiled. 'I had already inspected the houses at various stages with Nikos Nicolaides while they were being built.'

Her eyes flashed. 'Then you knew perfectly well mine would be suitable.'

'More or less,' he admitted, and filled her water glass.

'So will you drive me there this afternoon, please?'

Instead of answering, he greeted Eleni with a smile as she delivered a large dish giving off delicious scents. 'Ah, *garides saganaki*, or, for our English guest, prawns with feta in tomato sauce—and probably a few subtleties known only to the cook,' he announced. '*Efcharisto*, Eleni.'

'Eat while hot,' she instructed as she left.

'This smells heavenly,' said Isobel with anticipation.

Luke got up to take the bowl she filled for him. 'You like Greek food?'

'It's only my second experience of it. But,' she said, after tasting the prawns, 'this is just wonderful. I adore seafood.'

'Which is fortunate,' said Luke. 'I did not ask if you were allergic to shellfish.'

'I'm not. Nor to anything else, so far. I have a pretty iron digestive system normally.' She flushed. 'Which is why I was so mortified yesterday on the way down to the clinic. It was a new experience for me.'

'For me, also,' Luke said with feeling, and looked her in the eye. 'You are quite well now in that way?'

'Absolutely. Otherwise I wouldn't be tucking into this delicious prawn dish. Eleni's a great cook. Has she been with you long?'

'All my life. She helped my mother with me when I was a baby. Also her husband Spiro, the son of my mother's old nurse, Sofia. As I told you,' added Luke, 'everyone on Chyros knows my history.'

'That must be rather wonderful—like an extended family.'

He inclined his head. 'Which is why I spend as much time here as possible, when my work allows. In Athens and Thessaloniki many people know who I am, but few know the real Lukas Andreadis.'

'Do you prefer it that way?'

'In some ways, yes. But, like you, I have good friends—in my case, men whose interests are similar to mine.'

'You said your interest in women is well known, too,' she reminded him.

Luke looked her in the eye. 'But they are—or were—just pillow friends, Isobel. I always make my views on marriage—or even commitment—very clear.'

Her hackles rose. Why did he think it necessary to tell her that? She had no designs on him. Or on any other man for the foreseeable future. 'I thought a man like you would want a son to inherit this empire of yours. Not that it's any business of mine,' she added hastily.

'Do you want a husband and family, Isobel?' asked Luke, surprising her.

'Not right now, no.'

'You have never met a man you wish to marry?'

'No,' she said shortly, and smiled as Eleni appeared with a bowl of fruit. 'That was absolutely delicious,' she told her, indicating her empty dish.

The woman looked pleased as she cleared away.

'I saw Dr Riga when I was down in the town,' said Luke casually, once they were alone. 'He thinks it best you remain here at the villa for a few days, rather than manage alone at the cottage.'

Isobel stared at him in astonishment. 'But why? There's nothing wrong with me now, except for the foot. And with my crutch and this wonderful stick I'll be fine on my own.'

'Nevertheless, he advises you stay here until completely recovered.' He shrugged. 'After a fall on the head there can be complications.'

She frowned. 'What kind?'

'A clot of blood on the brain, for one. There was a case only recently of a young boy complaining of head pains after a fall. Lacking the necessary equipment, the doctor performed emergency surgery with an ordinary power drill to release the pressure on the brain and saved the boy's life.'

Isobel blanched, beginning to regret the prawns.

Luke smiled in reassurance. 'Since there was no fracture to your skull, Dr Riga said there is no risk of this in your case. But he thinks you should stay here for a while. So do I.' Though for a quite different reason. 'Eleni thinks so, too.'

Isobel drew in a deep breath, deeply shaken by the idea of blood clots. 'Poor Eleni. I've given her so much extra work.'

'She does not think of it that way, Isobel,' he assured her, peeling an orange. 'In fact, Eleni thinks you are a very lovely young lady, so does Spiro.' The dark, compelling eyes met hers for a moment. 'I agree with them.'

Isobel's eyes fell. 'Thank you. If I had to have an accident I was very lucky to land on your beach for it. You've all been so kind.'

'Including me?' he said, eyes gleaming.

Her chin lifted. 'Once you found I wasn't a journalist, yes, you were—are—kind. Autocratic, too, but I suppose that's second nature to you.'

'If I were truly autocratic,' he said very deliberately, 'I would simply *demand* that you stay here. But, even on such short acquaintance, Miss Isobel James, I realise that this would work against me. So, I repeat my invitation. Stay a little while longer.'

Isobel sighed. 'Now you've planted the idea of electric drills in my head, solitude at the cottage has no appeal right now. So thank you. I will stay for a day or so.'

'Very wise. And when you do leave the villa I shall arrange

for someone to check on you at regular intervals,' he stated, then arched an eyebrow as she smiled wryly. 'What is so amusing?'

'You were in touch with your inner autocrat again, Mr Andreadis.'

'I cannot help who—and what—I am.' Luke smiled. 'I return to Athens shortly, so you may convalesce here in peace, Isobel. And when you are ready to leave, Spiro will drive you to the cottage.'

CHAPTER FOUR

ISOBEL was much cheered by this piece of news. It would be a lot more peaceful at the Villa Medusa without the formidable presence of its owner. But she would miss him from a transport point of view.

'What is going on behind those beautiful blue eyes?' Luke asked, startling her. 'I can almost hear your brain working.' His eyes gleamed. 'Is it possible you might miss my help in carrying you downstairs?'

'Yes,' she said frankly.

'I had thought of that,' he informed her. 'I considered asking Milos to carry you when necessary. But I decided against it.'

'Why?'

Luke looked at her in silence for a while. 'Not a suitable solution,' he said at last. 'Instead, we shall transfer you to a room down here.'

Isobel eyed him curiously. 'May I ask why you didn't put me there in the first place?'

'It had no bed. Now it does. It will be much better for Eleni,' he added. 'It will save her from constant running upstairs to check on you.'

'A definite plus,' agreed Isobel meekly. 'Thank you.'

'Would you like to see the room now?'

'Yes, please.' She picked up the crutch and manoeuvred herself away from the table.

'It would be easier if I carried you,' he said, joining her.

'Unnecessary down here. I'm pretty nippy already with my trusty crutch,' she assured him. 'So lead on, Mr Andreadis.'

He conducted her back into the house and along the hall into a sitting room with glass doors leading on to the terrace and an awning outside to shield the room from the sun. Furniture had obviously been rearranged to allow for the bed to be placed with the best view of the garden.

Isobel looked round doubtfully. 'It's lovely, but isn't this where you sit at night?'

'Rarely. I prefer the conservatory, or my study on the other side of the hall. Sometimes I stay out on the terrace until I go to bed.' Luke smiled. 'Use the room as long as you wish, Isobel. The ground floor bathroom is close by. Eleni and Spiro have one of their own, so you are assured perfect privacy.'

Isobel examined her new quarters in silence. Her belongings were already arranged on the desk, and her clothes hanging on a dress rail beside it. 'I booked my holiday on the recommendation of a client who came here to recover from a divorce,' she said at last. 'She told me that Chyros was the perfect place for peace and quiet, but in my case she was wrong.'

Luke opened the doors onto the terrace. 'Why did *you* need peace and quiet? A love affair gone wrong?'

'No,' lied Isobel. 'My boss recently gave the gallery a huge makeover, and I had my work cut out to make sure it was business as usual during the alterations. At the same time I was working on a commission for a series of watercolours, and setting up an exhibition of paintings by an artist friend at the gallery for its ceremonial reopening.' She smiled wryly.

'Not quite the same high octane stuff as your takeovers, but I was glad of some time off once everything was sorted.'

'Then it is far better you stay here for a while and let Eleni and Spiro take care of you. You have a phone?' he added.

'Yes. At least I hope so.' She limped over to the desk and looked in her bag. 'Still here, thank goodness. In all the excitement yesterday it's a wonder I didn't lose that, too.'

'Give me your number,' he ordered, taking his phone from a pocket. He keyed the number into it, then held out his hand for hers. 'I shall enter mine in yours.'

'I shan't need it,' she said quickly.

'You might. I shall charge this before I give it back.' He gave her a searching look. 'Your head is aching?'

'Yes.'

'I can tell. I shall send Eleni with tea. Take some medication and rest for a while. I shall see you later at dinner,' he added as he left.

When Eleni came with the tea, Isobel asked directions to the bathroom and later, when she was propped up on the comfortable bed, looking out on the garden through the open doors, admitted that now the owner was leaving she had no objection to spending another day or two here. Talk of blood clots had given her quite a fright. On her own in the cottage, the slightest pain in her head would have sent her imagination into overdrive.

She leaned back with a sigh. Here at the Villa Medusa it would be dangerously easy to laze away the days of her holiday in true lotus-eating style, whereas part of her original intention for her trip to Greece had been to produce some watercolours she could put up for sale at the gallery on her return. Joanna had dismissed that idea out of hand, arguing that the idea of a holiday was to have fun as well as take a rest. But to Isobel painting *was* fun. So tomorrow, once Luke Andreadis had left for Athens, she would set up her water-colours, paint the pool in its frame of lush greenery and, if she considered the result good enough, leave it for him as thanks for his help. The help had been hostile and reluctant at first but he'd given it just the same, even though he'd mistaken her for a journalist, or worse. And, unless she was much mistaken, he still suspected her of stranding herself on his beach like some party girl after a good time. But the fact remained that he had rescued her, arranged medical attention and taken her into his home to recover. She owed him.

Isobel slept a little, and when she woke just lay there, savouring the pleasure of simply feeling better. But after a while she sat up and stealthily eased herself out of bed. With the help of the crutch she would go exploring. Moving with care, she went out onto the terrace, wishing she had her sunglasses. Hers, presumably, were still down on that beach somewhere. Pity. With growing confidence Isobel made her way along the marble flags edging the pool and stood looking into the water in longing for a minute or two, then with a sigh turned back towards the arcaded terrace surrounding the house. But, as she turned, the tip of the crutch stuck in a crack and with a shriek she fell onto the grass.

Instantly she was swept up in strong, unfamiliar arms and a flood of anxious Greek poured into her ears. Deeply embarrassed, Isobel tried to reassure Milos she was unhurt. Her face flamed as Luke strode out of the house, holding out imperious arms, and Milos hastily surrendered Isobel to his employer and picked up the crutch. He confirmed there was no damage to it and, with a brief word of thanks to Milos, Luke carried Isobel along the terrace and out of the sun.

She eyed his stern face warily. 'Sorry for the disturbance,' she said at last.

'Tell me the truth. Are you really unhurt?' he demanded.

'Yes. I fell on the grass—soft landing this time.' Her smile met with a stony look.

'And yet you are determined to go back to the Kalypso to manage alone!'

'But when I'm there I'll stay in the house,' she protested, and sighed. 'I just wanted to look at your beautiful garden.'

'You could have fallen in the pool!'

She shrugged. 'No problem. I'm a strong swimmer.'

'Excellent,' he said grimly. 'At least I shall not worry that you drown while I am away.' He turned away to the table to pour a glass of fruit juice for her, then perched on the edge of the table, scowling down at her while she drank it.

'Please apologise to Milos for me,' said Isobel.

Luke's mouth curved in a sardonic smile. 'No apology is necessary. Milos was no doubt grateful for the chance to hold you in his arms.'

Isobel eyed him incredulously. 'You think I fell on purpose?'

He gave a cynical shrug. 'Did you?'

She drank the rest of her ice-cold juice to calm down. 'No,' she said when she could trust her voice. 'I did not. Thank you for the drink. Now, if you'll excuse me?' She stood up and limped off to her new room, filled with a burning desire to assault Luke Andreadis with her crutch as he kept pace with her. She gave him a cold little smile as he opened the door for her. 'Thank you. Would you be kind enough to ask Eleni to see me when she has a moment?'

'Of course. Unless there is something I can do for you instead?' Luke eyed her challengingly when she shook her head. 'You are angry?'

'Not in the least,' she lied.

'No?' He arched a disbelieving eyebrow. 'I will fetch Eleni.'

'Thank you so much.'

Isobel stared out into the garden, fuming. Did Luke really imagine she'd fallen over just so that brawny Milos could pick her up? Or, even worse, so that the lord and master himself could come to her rescue again. She ground her teeth impotently. Luke had grabbed her away from Milos as though she were a parcel. Or baggage, from his point of view. She smiled reluctantly, her sense of humour reasserting itself as Eleni came rushing in.

'Isobel? You ill?'

'No, no, nothing like that. I feel fine.'

'Milos said you fell.'

'My crutch stuck in a crack and tripped me up.'

Eleni tutted disapprovingly. 'So what you need?'

'I hate to make extra work for you, but could I possibly have my supper in here on my own tonight?'

The woman looked anxious. 'You did hurt!'

'No, no. I'd just rather eat alone. Please?'

Eleni plumped up the pillows on the bed, eyeing her narrowly. 'You rest. Not time to eat yet.'

'*Efcharisto*, Eleni.'

Although she'd opted out of dining with the lord and master of Villa Medusa, an encounter with him later was no doubt inevitable. To armour herself for it, Isobel washed carefully in the bathroom and zipped herself into a cool cotton shift in her favourite cornflower-blue. With even more care, she combed out her hair, then subsided gratefully against the pillows on the bed. The crutch was a huge help, but getting around with it was tiring just the same. She longed to ring Joanna, but if she did Jo would immediately sense something wrong and keep nagging until Isobel confessed. Time enough for that when she went home. She closed her eyes against a sudden wave of homesickness. When she opened them again she saw Luke on the terrace, watching her through the open doors.

'May I come in?' he asked.

'It's your house.'

'But this is your room.'

She shrugged indifferently. 'Come in, if you want.' A pity to waste the primping.

Luke came to stand by the bed, looking down at her. 'Eleni says you refuse to join me for dinner.'

'Yes. I'd rather eat alone in here.'

'Why?'

She raised a disdainful eyebrow. 'You were insulting, Mr Andreadis.'

'It was a shock to see Milo holding you in his arms,' he said harshly. 'I thought you were hurt.'

'No,' she corrected. 'You thought I'd engineered a fall just so he'd pick me up.'

'Only for a second.' He smiled persuasively. 'Am I forgiven?'

In his dreams! 'Of course.'

'Then you will dine with me?'

'No, thank you.'

To Isobel's annoyance, Luke drew up a chair and sat down. 'Then I shall also eat here.'

This was silly! 'Eleni wouldn't approve of that,' she told him crossly.

'So join me on the terrace.' He was silent for a moment. 'I apologise, Isobel. My only excuse is my reaction to seeing you in Milos's arms.' His eyes locked on hers with a look which set alarm bells ringing again. 'I was angry when I saw him touching you.'

'How utterly ridiculous,' she said scornfully. 'Milos was just being kind.'

'You will discourage him from such kindness in future!'

Isobel glared at him. 'I will certainly make sure that neither he, nor you, Mr Andreadis, will be forced to pick me up again.'

'No force is necessary,' he assured her, his eyes gleaming, and took her hand. 'To hold you in my arms is a great pleasure, Isobel. Even though you make it so clear the pleasure is not mutual.' He smiled persuasively. 'Change your mind. Dine with me tonight. Otherwise, poor Eleni must serve a meal in two places. Three, if you count the one she shares with Spiro.'

Isobel gave in, defeated. Eleni had been so kind it was hardly fair to cause her extra work. And Luke would be gone soon. Even if he returned to Chyros while she was here, she would be at the cottage, not the villa. She detached her hand very deliberately.

'Oh, very well,' she said at last. 'But only to save Eleni.'

Luke smiled victoriously. 'Good. Rest until dinner time. I shall come for you later.'

Alone again, Isobel lay deep in thought as she gazed through the open doors at the sunlit garden. Luke was giving out signals she identified with misgivings. Was he expecting some kind of return for her bed and board? He was a danger-ously attractive man, not least for the inner force so plainly burning behind the impressive physical exterior. But she had no intention of indulging in anything remotely like a fling with him. Or any other man. Had he really been jealous just because Milos fielded her when she fell? She ground her teeth impotently. A very good thing he was leaving tomorrow. Otherwise, he might take her consent to stay on here as will-ingness to be his 'pillow friend', whatever that meant. It was not impossible. She was far from looking her best at the moment, but in her normal state men were usually attracted to her. With disastrous results in one instance. She shivered.

That there was no significant male presence in her life right now was entirely her own choice. And she was going to keep it that way.

Isobel would have given much to wash her hair, but instead settled for a careful session with a hairbrush, and application of eye-shadow and concealer that worked wonders on her rapidly fading bruise. In spite of all the drama, her headache was surprisingly absent, her ankle less painful and for just moving around the room she could manage with the walking stick. But she would play safe with the crutch to make for the terrace rather than wait for Luke to fetch her.

When he joined her at the dinner table, spectacular in dark linen trousers and a shirt in a shade of pink which looked outrageously good on him, Luke raised a quizzical eyebrow.

'I went to your room, but my little bird had flown away.'

Isobel smiled smugly. 'I needed the exercise.'

'While I had hoped for the pleasure of carrying you,' he assured her suavely, and seated himself beside her. 'Is your headache better?'

'Touch wood,' she said, tapping the table, 'it seems to have gone.'

'Excellent. In that case, will you have a glass of wine? A local label, but I think you will like it.'

'I'm sure I will. Thank you.'

'Thank *you*,' he said very deliberately, 'for joining me tonight after I made you so angry this afternoon.'

She eyed him through lowered lashes, her antennae on the alert in response to Luke Andreadis in charming mode. Why the change of attitude? She raised the glass he'd filled for her. 'You're leaving soon, so let's enjoy the evening in a spirit of friendship.'

Luke raised his own glass. 'We will enjoy the evening, certainly, but I shall return from Athens before you leave.'

'Will you? I thought you'd be too busy with your new venture.'

'I shall be. But I employ clever people more than capable of keeping the engines running when I take time off,' he assured her, and drank some wine. 'Even Air Chyros, my new baby, has a specialist department to look after it and can therefore function without me for short periods. So,' he added, 'should you have a problem, just ring me and I can arrange for whatever help you need. But if you feel ill in any way tell Spiro to contact Dr Riga immediately.'

'I'm sure I'll be fine from now on. But I appreciate the thought.'

'You value your independence very highly,' said Luke indulgently. 'Is there no man at all in your life, Isobel?'

Her eyes shadowed. 'No.'

He shook his head. 'Amazing. Why not?'

Isobel shrugged. 'Because I haven't met anyone remotely suitable lately.'

Luke's eyebrows shot into his hair. 'A cold attitude! A lover must be more than just suitable. Have you never met a man who makes your heart beat faster?'

Yes, but for entirely the wrong reasons. 'I was in a relationship quite recently,' she admitted.

He waited, but when Isobel merely drank her wine he stared at her in frustration. 'So what happened?'

'We broke up due to irreconcilable differences.' She shrugged. 'I wanted his friendship. He was fixated on my appearance. He just couldn't see past it to the personality—and hopefully brain—behind the hair and eyes.'

Luke frowned. 'But surely a man can be attracted by both your looks and your brain?'

'Very few, unfortunately.'

Luke offered her a plate of olives. 'You must eat well tonight to gain your strength. You are too thin, Isobel.'

'I'm sure you were glad of that when you were forced to carry me around so much!'

'Very true. Most ladies of my acquaintance are more generously built,' he admitted, and smiled into her eyes. 'In Athens I will think of you when you are eating alone here.'

Isobel shook her head. 'You'll be too busy.'

'Not too busy to think of *you*, Isobel,' he assured her, a gleam under the heavy, lazy lids she was getting to know. And suspect.

'Amazing!' she said, shaking her head in wonder.

'What is amazing?'

'How you've changed from the man who was so furious at finding me on his beach.' She eyed him curiously. 'If I had been just a sunbathing trespasser, instead of injured and unconscious, what would you have done?'

'My usual treatment is a harsh lecture, after which I give the trespasser a swift passage back to the harbour.' He eyed her thoughtfully. 'I *think* I would have done the same for you, but that is very hard to imagine. Now.'

'I'm sure you'd have sent me packing, just like the rest.'

He smiled indulgently. 'I doubt it.'

Isobel took refuge in her wine. Unless she was mistaken, Luke really was showing signs of fancying her as one of his 'pillow friends'. And because he'd rescued her from his beach and taken her into his home, he probably thought he had the right to expect it. Which would make for a very difficult situation when she refused. As she would.

'You're very quiet,' he commented.

'Anticipation of dinner. And here comes Eleni with it right now,' she added, relieved.

'Which I trust you will eat. Otherwise, you will be too weak to get back to your cottage before you fly home. Right, Eleni?'

The woman nodded vigorously. 'Much better stay here.' She patted Isobel's shoulder as she left.

'Eleni's very sweet,' said Isobel.

'I shall tell her you said so. She will be pleased—she has taken a great fancy to you.' He shrugged. 'I have never brought a woman here. She is enjoying the experience.'

To Isobel's irritation, this information pleased her. How silly was that? His social life was nothing to do with her. 'You keep that side of your life for Athens, I suppose?'

'That side of my life?'

'The pillow friends and so on.'

'By that particular term I mean those ladies who are happy to wine and dine and stay the night occasionally. I make my intentions clear from the start,' he added deliberately, 'so that no one is misled—or hurt.'

She seriously doubted that. Probably they all hoped that wining and dining—and a sleepover—would just be the opening bout for the main event of something permanent with a man like Lukas Andreadis, who possessed physical appeal, success and wealth as the triple layer of icing on the cake. A combination far too overpowering for Isobel.

After the meal Luke suggested she might like to sit in one of the reclining chairs beside the pool.

'I would, indeed—'

Before the words were out of her mouth, Luke picked her up and carried her along the terrace to lay her carefully in one of the chairs. 'Are you comfortable?' he asked as he straightened.

'Yes—thank you,' she said through clenched teeth, irritated to find that, while her brain repudiated physical intimacy with

Luke as total disaster, the fleeting physical contact with him had sent her hormones running riot, damn them.

'What is wrong, Isobel?' he asked, taking the chair beside her.

'Nothing. How could anything be wrong?' she said, getting a grip. 'It's so beautiful here.'

'True—' He groaned as his phone rang. 'Forgive me for a moment?' he asked, identifying the caller. 'I must answer this.'

'Of course.' Isobel watched him stride into the house, talking to his caller in tones which made it obvious, even though she couldn't understand a word of it, that the news he was being given was bad. She sat back in her chair, giving her hormones a stringent lecture as she watched the play of lights on the pool.

Luke looked grim when he rejoined her. 'I must leave for Athens at daybreak.'

'Trouble?'

'Of a kind, yes. During the airline takeover there was one solitary dissenter when the board voted for my acquisition.'

'And he's making difficulties for you?'

'She,' he corrected, with a harsh note in his voice that won him a sharp look. 'The woman previously in charge of the airline. When she found there was no way to stop the merger going through, the lady was so enraged she eventually suffered a stroke. I have just been informed that she died of it today.'

'Do you feel you're to blame?' asked Isobel soberly.

Luke looked at her in surprise. 'No. If the gods struck her down it was her fate.'

'That's very—Greek of you.'

He shrugged. 'Even if I am to blame for her stroke *and* her death, I am merely the instrument fate chose for this.'

Her eyes widened. 'You obviously didn't like her much.'

'Like her?' Luke gave a mirthless bark of laughter. 'It

may shock you to hear this, but I hated her so much I rejoice in her death.'

His brutal honesty sent shivers down Isobel's spine. 'Will you go to her funeral?'

'Of course. It will be expected. Funerals take place here as soon as possible after death, so tonight there will be the *Trisagion*, or vigil, with prayers for the departed. I would not have attended that even if I were there, but I shall put in the necessary appearance at the church tomorrow, complete with black arm band. Unless her husband turns me away at the door,' he added grimly.

'But if his wife had a stroke, it's hardly reasonable to blame you for her death!'

'He has never been a reasonable man.'

'You know him well?'

'I know *of* him well enough!'

'Was he involved in the takeover negotiations?'

Luke smiled coldly. 'For some reason he chose to stay behind the scenes and let his wife Melina do the talking, which was his big mistake. If he had conducted the negotiations himself, things might not have gone so well for me. But from the day he gave her nominal control of the airline, his wife made enemies of every man on the board. The result was unanimous acceptance of my offer.'

'Not a nice lady.'

Luke smiled grimly. 'Not nice at all, Isobel.'

'But her husband must be grieving for her, just the same.'

'Possibly. But he has many business interests to console him. I doubt he will grieve for long.'

'That's cold! You obviously don't like him, either.'

Luke's teeth showed white in the semi-darkness. '*Like* is too lukewarm a word, Isobel.'

'You know him well, then?'

'No. If I meet him tomorrow it will be for the first time. Yet Theodore Andreadis is my grandfather.'

CHAPTER FIVE

ISOBEL'S eyes widened in astonishment. 'Your *grandfather*? And you've never met him?'

'He does not acknowledge the relationship.' The words sounded like pebbles dropped in a dish. Luke shrugged. 'Not that I wish him to, nor do I trade on the fact that I am his grandson. To me, he is just a tyrannical old man I cannot forgive for his treatment of my mother. If I tell you what he did it may help you understand.' He turned to look at her. 'Though normally this is not a subject I discuss.'

'Your confidence is safe with me, I promise.'

'I do not doubt it. So, let me explain the rift. My grandmother, the first wife of Theo Andreadis, left him for a lover when their daughter was a baby, but died soon afterwards. To avoid history repeating itself, Theo brought Olympia up very strictly, educated at home instead of sent to school, and allowed contact with only one friend he considered suitable. In time he remarried and presented her with Melina, the archetypal wicked stepmother. She,' he added harshly, 'made life a living hell for the young Olympia.'

'So that's why you hated her!'

'There was worse to come. Coaxed by her friend to break out and go to a party, Olympia met a man there. Afterwards, having tasted freedom, Olympia stole out of the house at night to meet him as often as she could. Her absences went unnoticed, due to the discretion of loyal servants who adored Olympia. But I was the inevitable result of these secret meetings. When Melina found out about the pregnancy, she urged Theodore Andreadis to throw his daughter out of the house for disgracing his name, as her mother had done before her. So he did,' Luke added harshly.

Isobel eyed him in horror. 'How did your mother survive?'

'With the help of her faithful friend Chloe, she managed to get to her old nurse, here on Chyros, and begged a job from Basil Nikolaides in the kitchen of his taverna. After I was born she kept her job, saved everything she could for my education, and after school hours and at weekends I worked, too, usually as deck hand on one of the fishing boats. The jewels left to her by my erring grandmother were all my mother took with her from her home in Athens, and sales of these saw me through college and financed my MBA. But, to my great sorrow, my mother died before I began making money with my freighters.' Luke's mouth tightened. 'So you see why I have no love for Theo Andreadis; even less for his harpy of a wife.'

Isobel was silent for a while. 'When did you start thinking about revenge?'

His lips tightened. 'From the day I heard what happened to my mother.'

'It must have been hard for her to tell you.'

Luke shook his head. 'She did not. I had it all from old Sofia, who would have murdered Theo Andreadis with her own bare hands if she could, and Melina with him. I swore I would one day take my revenge. But not with murder, as Sofia thirsted for. I had something more subtle and painful in mind. Taking over the airline was the perfect revenge on

Melina because it was the ultimate humiliation for her. She was so incandescent with fury it is no surprise that she had a stroke afterwards. Nor am I hypocrite enough to pretend regret that she is dead.'

Isobel was silent as she stared out into the starlit night, feeling chilled to the bone.

'You are shocked?' he asked.

'Stunned, rather. It's like a Sophocles tragedy.' She turned to him. 'You've had your revenge on Melina, but what about your grandfather? Is his wife's death enough revenge for you, or do you have something different planned for him?'

'I did not plan Melina's death—fate did that for me. And no doubt it will do the same for Theo Andreadis one day without my help. Even though I have no love for him, I will not seek revenge on someone of my own blood,' Luke assured her and smiled faintly. 'Isobel, you have not asked me the all important question.'

'I wouldn't dream of asking you any questions at all,' she assured him. 'I'm gratified that you told a stranger like me even this much.'

'It is not normal dinner table conversation,' he agreed. 'But you must surely be curious about the identity of my natural father.'

'I'm only human, so of course I am,' she said frankly. 'But only if you want to tell me.'

To his surprise, Luke found that he did. 'Chloe, the friend who took Olympia to the party, had a brother who excelled at athletics. He introduced the shy Olympia to the gold medallist swimmer he brought home from college for the party. It was love at first sight for both of them. After a series of brief stolen meetings, arranged with help from the faithful Chloe, the secret lover left to train for his next championship, promising to return to marry Olympia straight afterwards.'

'I'm not going to like the next bit,' said Isobel with foreboding. 'He didn't come back, obviously.'

'No. His plane crashed.'

'Oh, Luke, that's so sad!'

He nodded sombrely. 'All she had of him were his gold medals and the son he gave her. Apparently, I resemble him very closely. And,' he added with a smile, 'I have always been a powerful swimmer.'

'I saw you in the pool.'

'I know, Isobel.' He chuckled softly. 'Were you impressed?'

'Yes,' she said honestly. 'Though very embarrassed when you caught me watching.' She gave a sudden yawn, more from nerves than weariness. 'Sorry.'

'You are tired. It is time you went to bed.' Deaf to her protests, he picked her up and carried her along the terrace to her room, finding that his senses were stirred by emotions he normally kept under rigid control—the direct result of sharing such personal information with Isobel. Combined with the scent and warmth of the slender body in his arms, they filled him with a sudden urgent need for the kind of solace only a woman could provide and, instead of setting her down on her feet he sat down in the armchair with her in his lap. 'When a man rescues a damsel in distress he deserves a reward, *ne*?'

She stiffened, pulling away in alarm. 'What kind of reward do you have in mind?'

'Just a goodnight kiss.'

Isobel shook her head vehemently, pushing him away in such frenzied rejection Luke got up, grim-faced, and laid her down against the pillows on the bed.

'Do not look at me like that,' he said harshly, staring down into her ashen face. 'I am not a rapist.'

'Maybe not.' She hugged her arms across her chest, unable to meet his eyes. 'But neither am I applying for the post of pillow friend.'

Luke stood utterly still for a moment. 'A word of advice, Isobel,' he said after a pause. 'Wait until asked to apply for such a post before you refuse.'

She burrowed into the pillows, burning with mortification as he strode through the open doors. Thank God he was leaving tomorrow. Before he came back—if he did come back while she was here—she would be at the cottage. With a gasp, she shot upright again as he reappeared from the terrace with her crutch.

'I will send Eleni with tea,' he said curtly.

'No! Please tell her I don't need anything tonight.'

'As you wish.' Luke gave her a formal nod. 'I leave early in the morning. I shall say goodbye now.'

'Goodbye.' Isobel pulled herself together. 'Thank you again for all your help.'

He shrugged negligently as he made for the door. 'It was nothing.'

Isobel slumped against the pillows, fighting the urge to cry her eyes out. But if she gave in to tears the headache would come back and, threat of blood clots or not, tomorrow she was determined to leave the Villa Medusa. She looked at her watch and groaned. It was still quite early and she was no longer tired. Quite the reverse. The brief episode had sent her into such a spin she would take some calming down if she was to get to sleep any time before morning.

Later, propped up against pillows ready for the night, Isobel felt better, grateful to her head for letting her read. At least she wouldn't have to lie awake all night, mulling over the mortifying episode with Luke. But she couldn't explain why she'd shied off like a frightened virgin. Although he'd surprised her with details about his background, her own experience was too new and raw to talk about to a man who was virtually a stranger. So if Luke had harboured any idea about a holiday fling it was better to nip it in the bud right now. She sighed heavily. The physical contact of carrying her about so much had been to blame, creating intimacy from the word go.

Isobel steeled herself to concentrate on her book. Then looked up in surprise as someone knocked on her door.

'Come in,' she called, expecting Eleni, her body instantly rigid as Luke came in and closed the door behind him.

'I saw your light.' He approached the bed, something in his eyes pressing her panic button again. 'I knew you were awake, Isobel. I brought your phone.'

'Thank you,' she said stiffly. 'I'd forgotten all about it. I was reading.'

'The phone was just an excuse.' He sat on the edge of the bed, frowning as she backed away. 'Isobel, did you really believe that I would force you? You are a guest in my house, and still recovering from an accident. Do you think I am such a monster?'

'No. I don't.' Her eyes fell.

'Thank the gods for that,' he said dryly. 'Then why such panic?'

She drew in a deep, unsteady breath. 'Bad experience lately.'

'A lover who refused to take no for an answer?'

'Something like that.'

Luke's eyes darkened. 'He hurt you?'

She nodded.

'Can you talk about it?'

'No.'

'Perhaps it would be good for you if you did.' He put a finger under her chin to turn her face up. 'Tell me, Isobel.'

She stared at him in indecision, then sighed wearily. Why not? It was supposed to be easier to confide in a stranger. 'I have this problem,' she began very quietly. 'Due to my lack of relatives, I tend to look for friendship and caring rather than heat and, well, sex, when it comes to relationships. A few months ago I met an artist whose work we put on display at the gallery. He became a regular fixture in my life, good company for meals and concerts and so on. But nothing more than that. But when we got back from what turned out to be our last evening together he asked to see my latest series of watercolours. They were still in my flat, so for the first time I invited him up there.' She pushed the hair back from her face. 'He mistook the invitation for something else entirely. I tried to fight him off, but he's a big man and things got rough.'

Luke's eyes smouldered into hers. 'He raped you, this friend?'

Her hands clenched. 'He had a good try. But I fought him so hard I managed to jab him with a stiletto heel in a place which put a stop to proceedings.' She shivered. 'But not before he hurt me badly. Psychologically as well as physically.'

He swore under his breath. 'It would have been even worse if he had succeeded. You could have been left with child.'

Isobel flushed, and shook her head. 'I have close friends—twin brothers who are both doctors—and, on their advice, I've taken the necessary precautions for years against that kind of accident.' She sighed, depressed. 'Up to that point I'd really thought Gavin was a true friend like the Carey twins. But it was the same old story. He just wanted to get me into bed. And I haven't had a good night's sleep since.' She shrugged. 'I've given up on men since then. Other than the friends I've known forever.'

'I rejoice to know it is not something I have done.' Luke smiled wryly. 'I was most cast down when you refused to eat with me earlier. My dinner invitations are usually accepted more eagerly.'

She gave a choked little giggle. 'I bet they are.'

His eyes lit up. 'That is better. You are even more lovely when you smile, Isobel. But, if I say so, you will accuse me of appreciating your beauty more than your intellect.'

She smiled. 'Since you've been so kind I'll make an exception in your case, Luke.'

'So we are friends again?' He smiled slyly. 'You said you like men who wish to be friends.'

'I do. Not that it matters. I'll be back in England soon.'

'It is not time for you to go yet. And I shall return here in a few days,' he went on, surprising her. 'After the funeral I will work very hard to make sure I get away. By then,' he added, 'you will be well again. So take care this week. No climbing down cliff paths even when your ankle is better. If you want to sunbathe on my beach, Spiro will take you over in the *Athena*. Spiro,' he repeated significantly, 'not Milos.'

She smiled wryly. 'Actually, I won't bother either of them, thanks just the same. I'll be quite happy to sit on my veranda at the cottage, and when I can I'll stroll down to the taverna to eat.'

Luke frowned. 'It would be more sensible to stay here, Isobel.'

Not if he was coming back. She shook her head. 'It's very kind of you, but I really must get back to the cottage. Before I do, have I your permission for a swim in your pool?'

'Wait until I return. I will swim with you,' he said quickly. 'Dr Riga is coming to check on you tomorrow, and you must do as he says, *ne*?'

'Yes,' she said, resigned.

'And when you return to the cottage, take both walking stick and crutch.'

'Absolutely.' Isobel held out her hand, but her smile faded as her eyes met his. There was sudden taut silence between them, then Luke pressed a kiss on the hand. He leaned nearer, his eyes intent on hers. 'Normally,' he said softly, 'I like my women dark and voluptuous. Unlike you, my little English friend.'

'I definitely don't tick your boxes,' she said, determinedly prosaic. 'My hair is fair—'

'Golden,' he corrected.

'And I'm not in the least voluptuous. Nor,' she said firmly, 'am I one of your women.'

'No? But I saved your life,' he reminded her, his voice deepening. 'In some cultures that means you belong to me now.'

'Not in my culture! Besides, you just wanted to throw me off your island at first. Not quite the same as saving my life, Lukas Andreadis.'

'Was it not? You were unconscious and your foot was caught in the rock. What would have happened to you if I had not found you? I was destined to rescue you, Isobel. It is useless to struggle against the fates.' He smoothed the hair back from her forehead, careful to avoid her wound as he twisted a curl round his finger. 'This hair of yours fascinates me, *hriso mou*.'

'What does that mean?'

'In this instance, golden one.' He smiled into her eyes. 'I would like your friendship, Isobel.'

If only she could believe him. 'Why did you come back, Luke?'

'I had a brainwave, *ne*? Your phone!' He chuckled as he played with her hair. 'It was the perfect excuse. But now I must go.' Even though he wanted to stay. Whatever her motive for landing on his beach, he had a sudden desire to lie with her like this all night, hold her close and keep her safe, a discovery which shot Luke upright in panic. She was meant to be a diversion, not a complication in his life. Which had complications enough already. 'Goodnight,' he said abruptly, and made for the door.

'Goodnight,' said Isobel, surprised by his sudden hurry.

He opened it and turned, his eyes holding hers. 'Sleep well.'

As he went upstairs to his room Luke smiled wryly. His plan to charm his little golden bird into bed was not progressing according to plan, exactly. But she could not escape the fate that had sent her to him. His mouth twisted. He had spent too much of his life in plotting revenge to have much softness left in his psyche. His relationships with women were always transitory affairs to satisfy his male needs, with no emotions involved. But this English rose touched him in ways new to him. It was surprisingly vital for his peace of mind that she remained safe and well cared for at the villa rather than return to the Kalypso and risk relapse from her injuries. And he was only too willing to be Isobel's 'friend' for the short time they would have together before he let his little bird fly away.

So close a friend that soon he would make love to her with all the subtlety and skill at his command and erase all bad memories of men from her mind forever.

CHAPTER SIX

ISOBEL had barely closed her eyes before the sound of the helicopter woke her next morning. As she listened to it chop its way up into the sky above the villa she was thoughtful. He'd taken her rejection far better than expected. Not that one solitary 'no' from a woman he'd only known five minutes was likely to upset a man so comfortable in his own skin; especially smooth, bronzed skin that sheathed a muscular body so appealing to women he probably had to beat them off with a stick. And, with the kind of day he had in front of him today, he had probably forgotten her the moment he'd taken off into the sky. Yet now he'd gone the Villa Medusa felt oddly empty.

Eleni brought breakfast earlier than usual. 'Helicopter wake you, *ne*? I go shopping today,' she announced.

Isobel smiled cajolingly. 'Eleni, if I give you money, would you mind buying some food for me to take to the cottage? I'm going back there tomorrow.'

Eleni was dead against this idea and said so in all the English she had at her command, but Isobel was adamant.

'You've been so kind, but I'm giving you far too much work. If Spiro will drive me there tomorrow I'll be fine.'

'Dr Riga comes today,' said Eleni firmly. 'He must say.

Then I buy food. And now you must eat, Isobel. *Kyrie* Luke said I must take care of you.'

This information pleased Isobel more than she cared to admit as she mapped out her programme for the day while she ate her breakfast. Before Dr Riga came she would enjoy a proper shower. And later she planned to settle herself on the shaded part of the terrace to paint, so she could leave the watercolour of the pool for Luke as a permanent reminder of his trespasser.

To begin on her programme she removed the ankle bandage and the dressing on her temple, then turned on the shower. It was wonderful to stand under a warm spray and get totally clean, and she stayed under it so long Eleni was banging on the door before she'd finished.

'Come in,' Isobel called. 'It's not locked.'

Eleni hurried in, frowning in disapproval at the discarded bandages.

'I had to take them off. I just had to get clean, Eleni.' Isobel moved the foot experimentally. 'It feels a lot better. I thought I'd go outside—let the sun dry my hair a bit before it gets too hot.'

Dr Riga arrived soon afterwards. '*Kalimera*, Miss James,' he said, smiling. 'Lukas asked me to check on you before I start my clinic. How are you feeling?'

'Much better.' Isobel indicated her damp hair. 'I had a proper shower for the first time this morning.'

'You have made good progress.' The doctor took her pulse, then examined her face and bent to probe her ankle. 'I shall strap this up again to give support,' he told Isobel, 'but your head wound needs no more dressing; it is healing well.'

When Dr Riga had finished he gave a few more instructions, but agreed that she could return to the holiday cottage next day on condition that she was careful.

When he'd gone Isobel stood up and, with the aid of the crutch, took a few confident steps, delighted with the ankle in its smaller, neater strapping. She collected her bag of drawing materials and went back to the terrace.

'You see, Eleni?' said Isobel jubilantly when the woman brought coffee. 'Dr Riga says I can manage quite easily at the cottage now, so if Spiro will be kind enough to drive me I'll move back there tomorrow.'

The woman sniffed. 'Then I come to cottage every day. Make sure,' she said, eyeing the bag with suspicion. 'What you do with that?'

'I'm going to paint a picture for Luke as a present,' Isobel informed her, and won a broad smile of approval.

'Good, good,' said Eleni. 'Spiro drives me to shop now, Isobel, but Milos will guard you.'

Like the crown jewels, thought Isobel, amused. She drank her coffee while she laid out her drawing materials, then made a couple of trips to the bathroom to fill her water pots, delighted with her new mobility. She set up the light folding easel she'd brought with her and wetted the first sheet of paper. Even in the relatively temperate heat of early morning the paper had dried taut as a drum by the time she'd mixed her first batch of paints, and she was able to lay down her first background wash. The drying time was so much quicker than at home it was exhilarating to put down wash after wash at such speed. By the time Eleni and Spiro returned the background of her painting was well under way, but Isobel was flagging and glad to sit down.

She smiled as the couple came to check on her. 'You were quick!'

Spiro shook his head, smiling. 'We were long time, Miss Isobel.'

'I didn't notice!'

'Milos say he looked from garden, but you worked all the time,' said Eleni, her eyes admiring on the watercolour. 'You are so clever. Kyrie Luke will like very much, Isobel.'

'I hope so. But don't tell him what I'm doing. It's a surprise.'

'You hungry now?'

Isobel nodded with enthusiasm.

'How is your foot, *kyria*?' asked Spiro, picking up the coffee tray.

'Much better. Soon I'll be able to manage without the crutch.'

'Not today,' said Eleni firmly.

Isobel's phone rang as she was about to get back to work after lunch.

'How are you today, little friend?'

'Luke! Where are you?'

'In the car, on the way to the funeral. Has Dr Riga been to see you?'

'Yes. He's strapped my ankle again, and says I'll be fine on my own now.'

'I shall ring you tonight,' he promised. 'Rest this afternoon, Isobel. I wish…' But whatever Luke wished was lost in a burst of static.

Luke's sombre dark suit matched his mood as he arrived at the church shortly after the priest had received the grieving widower and family with the coffin at the front door. Theo Andreadis ignored Luke, but Zena and Zoe Karras, sisters of the dead Melina, eyed him with open venom behind their brother-in-law's back. Luke stared them out, then slipped into the back of the church after the cortege entered and prepared to endure the ceremony, his face a rigid mask as he listened

to the white-robed priests intoning prayers for forgiveness
and repose of the soul of the departed. What soul? thought
Luke savagely.

When the interminable service was over at last he was the
first to leave, in such a hurry to avoid his grandfather that the
man who hurtled out of the crowd with upraised knife took
him by surprise. Luke's lightning reflexes sent him ducking
sideways and the glancing blade pierced the sleeve of his
jacket to cut his arm as he slammed his fist into the assailant's
stomach, then, with a swift upper cut to the jaw, sent the man
sprawling on the ground. Suddenly there were women
screaming and police everywhere. Luke caught sight of his
grandfather's shocked face, but it was the gloating eyes of the
Karras sisters that remained with him afterwards, not least
because the gloating changed so quickly to furious disappointment. That he was still alive, obviously. He shot a cold,
scathing smile at the women, then turned away to the police
officers waiting to question him. Ambulances came rushing
to the scene, but he held the paramedics off, determined to
give all help possible to the police before he allowed anyone
to attend to his wound.

Inspired by talking to Luke, Isobel quickly immersed herself
in her painting. The noon light was brighter, more vivid than
before, and she spent a long time mixing paints to capture the
play of sunlight on the pool. Its frame of greenery was equally
challenging. The lush plant life seemed to encompass every
shade of green, with overtones of blue and vivid splashes of
contrast colour from tamarisk, oleander and geranium; a challenge she responded to with her usual concentration.

When Eleni coughed tactfully, rattling a tray, Isobel looked
up, blinking owlishly, and smiled.

'Drinks—wonderful; I'm thirsty.'

'Isobel, you have visitor.'

Isobel stared in surprise. 'Really? Who?'

'Alyssa Nicolaides. No worry. She speak English.'

'How very nice.' Isobel sat back in her chair, rotating her neck as she stretched. 'A break would be good. Could you bring her in while I have a wash?' She waggled her stained fingers and went off with her crutch to change her paint-spattered T-shirt and do something to her face and hair.

When Isobel got back to the terrace a young woman with a mass of dark curling hair spun round from an intent study of the watercolour and smiled warmly.

'Hello. I'm Alyssa. I was speaking to Dr Riga today, and he said you might like some company now Luke's gone.'

Isobel smiled back, delighted. 'I would, very much. How kind of you. Now I can thank you for packing my clothes.'

'I was glad to help. Alex told me about your accident.'

'Your brother was very kind, too. Please thank him when you speak to him again. Is he back at the hospital now?'

'Yes. He was just here for his days off.' Alyssa gestured to the painting. 'I'm impressed. You have enormous talent.'

'Thank you. How about some fruit juice, or water?'

'The juice will be fine. Shall I pour some for you?'

Isobel nodded. 'Please. Do sit down—I've been standing too long.'

Alyssa eyed the strapped ankle doubtfully as she pulled up a chair. 'Will you be able to manage at the cottage on your own?'

'Once Spiro drives me there, yes. The cottage is all on one floor, so with my crutch and the walking stick Luke gave me, no problem.' Isobel eyed her guest with interest. 'You speak very good English.'

'We had a marvellous English teacher here in school. I also

studied it along with my business degree, and went to work in England. I was there for several years.' Alyssa grinned. 'The accent is still strong, but I pride myself I'm fluent.'

'You certainly are. What did you do?'

'I worked in a London bank, with all those hotshot City boys.' She fluttered her eyelashes. 'One of them even tried to persuade me to share his trendy riverside apartment.'

With those eyes and curves and the luxuriant hair, Isobel could well believe it. Alyssa was probably exactly the type of woman Luke usually went for. 'But it didn't happen?'

'No. He was a charmer, and I was tempted, but I was homesick. By that time I had saved a fair sum of money, so home I came. Soon afterwards my baby brother introduced me to a handsome surgeon at his hospital.' She waggled a hand adorned with an impressive ring. 'And in a few weeks I'm going to marry my Dimitri. In the meantime I keep my English up with tourists at the taverna. But that's enough about me. Tell me about you.'

Alyssa listened, fascinated, as Isobel described her painting commissions and her job at the gallery, then bluntly asked her opinion of Luke. 'He's a great guy. Do you like him?'

'Yes. He's been very kind.'

Alyssa gurgled. 'How very British and restrained.'

Isobel felt her colour rise. 'Actually, he wasn't kind at all at first. He was downright menacing when he thought I was one of the paparazzi, lying in wait for him on his beach. But once I put him right about that he's been very—hospitable. But I can't trespass on his hospitality any longer.' She looked up in alarm as Eleni came rushing in, wailing and incoherent, and Alyssa jumped up, firing questions at the woman.

'Grab your crutch, Isobel,' she said tersely. 'There's a

television in Luke's study. Eleni saw an incident in Athens on the news.'

They hurried across the marble hall into a room full of electronic equipment. Alyssa gently pushed Isobel into a comfortable chair and switched on Luke's vast flat screen television.

'I heard Luke's name. Did Eleni say he was involved?' Isobel demanded, breathless from the rush.

'She wasn't making much sense. We'll find out more on here. Ah, here we go. Breaking news.'

The television showed a scene of noisy chaos, with police holding back crowds in front of a church. A reporter at the scene was giving an excited running commentary as paramedics loaded a stretcher into an ambulance. Isobel grasped Alyssa's hand urgently.

'What's happening?'

'Someone attacked Luke as he came out of church after the funeral of Melina Andreadis, his grandfather's wife. You knew about that?'

Isobel nodded impatiently. 'Go on.'

Alyssa listened again, then in rapid monotone translated the reporter's account. 'The grieving widower, accompanied by his dead wife's sisters, watched in shock as Lukas Andreadis, successful entrepreneur, knocked the attacker to the ground even though wounded himself—'

'Wounded?' Isobel swallowed, but forced herself to keep quiet as Alyssa listened intently before translating.

'Luke has been admitted to hospital for treatment. The body on the stretcher was the assailant. Luke obviously flattened him.' Alyssa let out a deep breath, then turned to Eleni, who was weeping in Spiro's arms, her eyes fixed in anguish on the screen. Alyssa patted her hand and soothed her with a flood of comfort in her own language, then took a phone from the pocket of her tangerine linen skirt.

'I'll get in touch with Dimitri at the hospital, or Alex if not. Don't worry. I'll soon find out about Luke.' She frowned. 'Are you all right, Isobel? You're very pale.'

'Startled, that's all. Never mind me—make your calls.'

Alyssa went off with her phone, giving succinct instructions which sent Eleni hurrying off to the kitchen while Spiro escorted Isobel back to the terrace.

'Do not fear, Miss Isobel,' said Spiro. 'Lukas is very strong man.'

'Yes, of course.' Isobel took in a deep breath and smiled brightly. 'I'm fine. You comfort poor Eleni. She's terribly upset.'

'She loves Lukas like a son,' he said quietly. 'I, also.'

'I know that. So please don't bother about me,' said Isobel guiltily. 'I shouldn't be here, giving you extra work at a time like this.'

'*Kyrie* Lukas told us to take care of you.' Spiro patted her hand for the first time. 'It is our pleasure, not work. Eleni is making tea for you.'

The moment Spiro was out of sight Isobel knuckled tears away impatiently and fished in her bag for tissues. The knock on her head had obviously shaken something loose. She'd cried more since she came to Chyros than she had in years. But any news of Luke would be in Greek, which meant she was forced to wait in frustration until someone told her what was happening. Luke's first meeting with his grandfather had certainly been dramatic.

Isobel stared out at the garden, tense as a drawn bow as she waited for what seemed like years before Alyssa came rushing back to the terrace.

'Sorry to take so long. It took a while to get through to

either of them. Luke is fine!' She seized Isobel's hand in a grasp which made her wince. 'Just a small cut and some grazes and a black eye, according to Dimitri, but it was a text, so I don't have any details. Alex will ring later with more news.' She bent to give Isobel a sudden hug. 'There. Don't cry. Or maybe you should. Do you good. Now I must tell Eleni and Spiro.'

'Thank you,' said Isobel gruffly and blew her nose. 'Lord knows why I'm crying.'

'I can guess!' Alyssa gave her a saucy, knowing grin and ran off down the hall to the kitchen.

Isobel shivered suddenly. If the assailant had a knife, Luke had been very brave—or foolhardy—to attack him. She seized her crutch and made for the bathroom to wash her face, then joined Alyssa on the terrace, smiling ruefully. 'I just wish I understood Greek. It's nerve-racking being unable to understand what's happening.'

Alyssa eyed her challengingly, her big dark eyes sparkling. 'You really like Luke, I think.'

'I do now.' Isobel made a face. 'But I loathed him at first because he was so insulting. He took it for granted I was the kind of female who strands herself on his beach hoping for a fun time with him at the villa.'

'Poor Luke,' said Alyssa, laughing. 'With his looks, women have swarmed around him all his life, and now he's so successful it's even worse. But he never brings anyone with him to the island, Isobel. This is his retreat, and the locals respect his privacy.' She looked round with appreciation. 'You like the house?'

'Who wouldn't?' On impulse, Isobel reached out and touched the other girl's hand. 'I'm so glad you came today. It would have been hell with Eleni and Spiro too upset to speak English. If you feel like popping in at the cottage once I'm back there, please do.'

Alyssa grinned mischievously. 'I have instructions to "pop in" every day.'

Isobel sat back, startled. 'Who from?'

'Luke, of course. I'm to report to him if you need anything. Luke and I are old friends. We were in school together when we were young.'

Isobel eyed her narrowly. 'Were you and Luke ever more than friends?'

'No.' Alyssa shook her head. 'He was always too busy either studying or earning money any way he could to have time for girls at that stage. He looked me up in London when he was doing his MBA, but my boyfriend at the time took one look at my gorgeous old school pal and created hell. So Luke kept away.'

'But you're the type he goes for.'

'How do you know that?'

'He told me. Blondes leave him cold.'

'Until he met you, obviously.' Alyssa threw out a hand. 'I think he must be pretty hot for *you*, Isobel. Otherwise, why would he order his team to take such care of you?'

'Team?'

'Team Lukas, which means Eleni, Spiro, Milos and me, not to mention Dr Riga. We all have our instructions to take care of you. Talking of which,' said Alyssa, suddenly very serious, 'would you like me to come back this evening in case there's any news?'

Isobel could have kissed her. 'Oh, *would* you? Have dinner with me—but won't you be missed at the taverna?'

'Papa won't mind in the circumstances. He's very fond of Luke. And I won't be seeing Dimitri until the weekend.'

Alyssa looked at her watch. 'I'll go back and talk to my parents, then give them a hand for a couple of hours and come back here about eight.'

'Thanks a lot. I'll tell Eleni.'

'I'll send her to you on my way out. And don't worry. It would take a lot more than a few cuts and grazes to put Luke out of action!'

Once her vivacious visitor had rushed away, Eleni hurried out to Isobel.

'You all right?' she said huskily.

'I'm fine. How are *you*?'

'Better now. Is good for you Alyssa comes back. I make nice dinner.'

'All your dinners are nice—more than nice, they're fabulous.' Isobel reached out her hand and Eleni took it. 'Don't worry. Luke will be fine.'

The woman nodded. 'Spiro said. But I always worry.' She smiled shyly. 'Spiro and I never have children, but we helped *kyria* Olympia with her baby.'

'So he's like the son you never had,' said Isobel softly.

Eleni nodded and brushed a tear from her eye. 'I go now and cook. If any news on TV Spiro will say.'

The light had changed so much Isobel decided against any more work on the watercolour until next day. With an early start in the morning she could easily finish the painting before she left. She saw to her brushes, then sat staring out at the garden, deeply shaken by the thought that Luke could have been killed. Which was worrying. It would be madness to let her emotions get involved when she would never see him again once she left Chyros. But when her phone rang, relief flooded her in a joyous wave at the sound of Luke's voice.

'Isobel?'

'*Luke!* Are you all right? I saw the news. How badly are you hurt? Are you still in the hospital—?'

'Let me speak and I will tell you! Did Eleni tell you what happened?'

'No, she was in such a state she couldn't speak English. Spiro, too. But luckily Alyssa had come to see me, so the four of us watched the TV in your study, with Alyssa translating the newscast. Good God, Luke, you could have been killed!'

'Would you have mourned for me, Isobel?'

'Of course I would,' she said crossly. 'How long will you be in hospital?'

'I am not in hospital. I left straight after treatment. The man did less damage than he intended. I was too quick for him,' he added with arrogance, which made her smile.

'Stitches?'

'No, just dressings. And injections to counter possible infection from the blade.'

'Do you know the man?'

'No—' He cursed under his breath. 'Forgive me, Isobel, Andres wants me. I must go.'

No longer tired, Isobel sat at the desk and, desperate for something other than Luke to occupy her mind, began writing postcards. Picturing the effect on Jo if she gave a truthful account of her adventures on Chyros, she wrote the expected things about the beautiful island and the wonderful weather, then exchanged pen for walking stick and went off to smarten herself up before the stunning Miss Nicolaides came back.

Isobel heaved a sigh as she made for the bathroom. There was such an electric sparkle about Alyssa it was hard to believe that she and Luke had never been more than friends. Though Luke probably knew a lot of women like Alyssa—

vivid, voluptuous Greek beauties far more to his taste than skinny blonde Brits. Isobel laughed at her reflection when she caught herself pouting. Just like Jo's little sister Kitty when she couldn't get her own way. She did her best with her face, pleased that a touch of foundation made the bruise barely noticeable, and her newly washed hair shone, with lighter streaks here and there from the hours she'd spent baking on Luke's beach. Not too bad. How she'd envied Jo's thick straight bob when they were teenagers. And Jo had laughed her to scorn, full of envy for her friend's blonde curls. Barbie doll fixation, she'd teased, then dodged when 'Barbie' started throwing things. Ready at last in a raspberry-pink shift, Isobel went back to the terrace to help Eleni lay the table.

The woman smiled in approval. 'You look very pretty, Isobel!'

'Why, thank you, Eleni. I heard from Luke,' she added as she put out the silver, and the woman nodded happily.

'He ring Spiro. Is bad he not stay long in hospital.'

Isobel smiled. 'He doesn't like hospitals!'

Eleni shot her a knowing look. 'You like him, *ne*?'

Isobel coloured slightly. 'Of course. He's been very kind to me.'

'He likes *you*. He never bring woman here before.'

'He didn't bring *me*, Eleni. He was forced into helping me because I hurt myself.'

'He likes you,' the woman repeated firmly, then hurried away at the sound of a car.

In white palazzo trousers and a sea-green silk shirt which displayed enviable honey-toned cleavage, Isobel's visitor looked even more stunning than before.

'You look a lot better—nice dress.' Alyssa pulled up a chair. 'Recovered from the shock, Isobel?'

'More or less. Luke rang me. He left the hospital as soon as he'd been treated.'

'So I heard.'

Isobel shivered. 'Any news about the man who did it?'

Alyssa shook her head. 'The police are questioning him.'

'Will there be anything on the news right now?'

'The main newscast is on later, after our meal. I'll play interpreter much better once I've eaten.' Alyssa cast an eye over Isobel. 'Are you slim like that because you work at it?'

'No. Metabolism.'

'Lucky you. I have to watch my weight like a hawk.'

'What for?' Isobel eyed her blankly. 'You're gorgeous.'

'Thank you, *glykia mou!* But to stay that way I *do* have to work at it.'

'To please Dimitri?'

Alyssa smiled like a cat with the cream. 'No, he loves the curves. But I want to fit into my wedding dress. I brought a box of pastries with honey and nuts for dessert, by the way, but I'll limit myself to one only.'

'Sounds wonderful.'

'I brought a bottle of wine, too—a gift from my father. He says a glass of wine is good medicine in times of stress.' Alyssa put out a hand to touch Isobel's. 'Don't worry. Luke is a supremely fit man. He'll be fine.'

Isobel flushed. 'I'm concerned, Alyssa, that's all. Luke came to my rescue and I'm grateful to him, and I hate to see him hurt. But there's nothing going on between us. We've only just met.'

'An hour—a minute—is all it takes to fall in love—or lust, Isobel. But I won't tease any more. Here comes dinner.'

Entertained by Alyssa's account of her preparations for her wedding, Isobel ate well enough to satisfy Eleni when she came to clear away, but by then she could wait no longer. She looked at her guest in appeal. 'Would you check the news for me now, please?'

Alyssa promptly jumped up and handed Isobel her crutch to make for Luke's study. She brought up the required television programme, then patted Isobel's hand as a shot of Luke came on the screen.

'He's been discharged from hospital after treatment, and the assailant is in police custody,' reported Alyssa.

'That's it?' said Isobel, as a shot of schoolchildren filled the screen.

Alyssa nodded and turned the set off. 'If I hear anything more I'll let you know tomorrow. When do you intend leaving the villa?'

But Isobel had taken time to think this over. 'Perhaps I'll wait one more day after all. At the Kalypso I'll be cut off from any news. At least here I've got Eleni and Spiro to keep me up to speed.'

Alyssa nodded in warm approval as they returned to the terrace. 'Very wise. You'd be a bit isolated up there. Take my advice, stay on here until you're really mobile.'

'Et tu, Brute?' said Isobel wryly.

'No use spouting Latin to me, *kyria*, I'm Greek! And,' she added in sudden inspiration, 'you're a Brit so you're bound to like tea. Shall I ask Eleni to make some for us? I'll mention your change of plan.'

Isobel laughed and threw up her hands. 'All right, all right, I give in, *KYRIA* Nicolaides. I'll stay on here for a day or two more.'

'Be sure to tell Luke I was the one who persuaded you—he'll owe me!'

* * *

By Greek standards they'd eaten early. But, after Alyssa left to drive home with a message of thanks to her father for the wine, Isobel got ready for bed, suddenly exhausted. She settled herself against stacked pillows with a book, the usual tray of drinks left beside her by Eleni. But, instead of reading, she kept thinking of how near Luke had come to death that day, and frowned. Why did that matter so much? Just a short time ago she'd actively disliked him, but somewhere along the line her feelings towards him had undergone a sea change. Whatever the reason, Isobel gave a great sigh of relief when Luke rang.

'Did I wake you, Isobel?'

'No. How are you?'

'In terrible pain,' he said promptly. 'I need a friend to comfort me.'

'No, seriously—'

'I am serious. Are you in bed?'

'Yes.'

'I need a picture of you as I lie in my own, so tell me what you sleep in.'

She chuckled. 'A knee-length blue T-shirt. I go for comfort, not glamour in bed.'

'Glamour enough for me—' He drew in a sharp breath.

'What's wrong?' she demanded.

'My various scrapes and scratches making themselves felt. Sleep well, Isobel.'

She closed her phone slowly, then turned out the light and slid lower in the bed, yawning. For some reason, just hearing Luke's voice had been enough to settle her down to sleep. Hoping it had worked the same way for him, she stretched luxuriously and turned her face into her pillows.

* * *

Isobel continued work on her watercolour next day, inter-
rupted at intervals by brief phone calls from Luke.

'I am very glad you decided to remain at the villa. Wait
there until I come back. Please, Isobel,' he added, which was
so obviously an afterthought she grinned.

'I'll see,' was all she would promise, and said nothing
about her intention to complete not only the watercolour of
the pool before she left, but another of Luke's beach to go with
it. This was more difficult to accomplish when Eleni and
Spiro learned what she had in mind, since it meant a lot of
argument about working out of doors. But in the end Milos
rigged up a canopy to shade Isobel from the sun as she worked
at the cliff edge. The study of the pool was for Luke to remind
him of her in future. The painting of the beach was for herself,
who would need no reminders.

Isobel received a flying visit from Alyssa before the evening rush at the taverna, and added her bit to the concerns
voiced by Eleni and Spiro.

'Are you sure you should be doing this? Though it's very
beautiful,' said Alyssa, peering over her shoulder. 'Is that for
Luke, too?'

'No. This one's for me.'

'How's the ankle?'

'Much better. I'm really speedy with my faithful crutch!
It's good exercise, getting in and out of the house for bathroom
breaks. And, before you ask, I'm smothered in suncream and
I'm drinking gallons of water and eating whatever Eleni puts
in front of me. But thank you for coming, Alyssa.'

'My pleasure. Alex sends his regards, by the way. He saw
Luke when he was at the hospital and assures you he's fine.'

Isobel raised an eyebrow. 'Why should Alex assure *me*?'

Alyssa fluttered her eyelashes. 'Who knows? Now, be good

and I'll come back tomorrow. We'll have extra help then, so I can stay longer. If you like.'

'I'd like that very much! Thanks a lot, Alyssa.'

After concentrating for hours to make use of the light, Isobel was very tired by the time Spiro helped Milos take down the canopy. 'Time to stop, *kyria*,' he said severely, taking charge of her painting materials. 'Now you rest, then eat good dinner.'

It was a programme Isobel was only too glad to follow. She had a long shower, but felt so tired halfway through the meal she gave up and let Eleni help her to her room, scolding all the way because Isobel had been too weary to eat.

'I bring tea,' said the woman as they reached the room. 'You go to bed now, *ne*?'

'Yes, Eleni,' Isobel promised meekly, startled to feel suddenly cold in the evening breeze coming through the veranda doors. Shivering, she searched in her suitcase for a pair of leggings to go with her vest, and even pulled tennis socks over feet that were suddenly icy.

'Too much sun, work too hard,' said Eleni sternly when she returned with the tea. 'You want blanket?'

'No, I'll be fine now, thank you. Goodnight, Eleni.' Isobel drank the hot tea gratefully and settled back against the pillows.

Luke rang before she had time to wonder if he would. 'How are you, Isobel?'

'I'm in bed now, but I've had a busy day. I've been painting.'

'I heard this. Out on the cliff edge,' he said sternly.

'I wanted a painting of the beach to take home as a souvenir.'

'To remind you of Chyros—and me? I need no reminders,' he said softly. 'I shall never forget my beautiful trespasser.'

Good, thought Isobel, who had painted the watercolour with just that end in view. 'How are your scrapes and scratches?'

'Healing fast.'

'Do you know why the man attacked you?'

'Yes.' His voice hardened. 'After much persuasion, he told the police he was paid to wound me but not to kill. He insists he has no idea who paid him, but I refuse to believe this. The man is obviously too frightened to name names. He said the money and instructions were delivered to him by courier, along with threats to harm his children if he refused.'

'Then, for heaven's sake, take care, Luke,' warned Isobel, startled. 'Whoever paid him might find someone else to hurt you even more. Is there good security where you live?'

'The best. The building I live in has every security device known to man. I have excellent security staff, also temporary police protection. But as soon as I can I shall return to Chyros, where no hurt ever comes to me.'

CHAPTER SEVEN

IT WAS a long time before Isobel slept. She felt worried because Luke was in danger, and even more worried because she felt that way. Don't go there, she warned herself forcibly. She was just about getting over the recent hateful episode. Only a fool would lay herself open to more emotional trauma. Especially with a man who lived his life to a very different set of rules from hers. She tossed and turned endlessly, but when heavy, exhausted sleep overtook her at last she was jolted out of it into a waking nightmare by rough hands which dragged her out of bed, her terrified scream smothered by a pungent cloth clamped over her face.

When Isobel opened her eyes again she felt icy-cold as she stared up into a starlit sky. She could hear an insistent put-putting noise, but instead of fear her knee-jerk reaction was sheer bloody-minded anger when she found she was tied up. Other people had nice package holidays, uneventful except for lost luggage, plane delays and sunburn, while so far hers had been one disaster after another. But burning resentment swiftly morphed into the cold chill of fear as she identified the noise. It was an outboard motor and she was not only in the bottom of a boat, but trussed up like an oven-ready chicken. How long had she been unconscious? And where on earth was she being taken? Even more frightening, what would happen when she got there? At least the smothering cloth had gone. Chloroform, probably. She swallowed down on a wave of nausea, thankful she hadn't been gagged, then clenched her teeth in anguish as she prayed hard that nothing had happened to Eleni and Spiro. And, instead of howling in anger at fate, she forced herself to lie perfectly still. Better to pretend she was still unconscious than risk the chloroform treatment again.

But why had she been snatched? If ransom was the motive, she had no money so she was no earthly use to a kidnapper. She shivered, feeling cold for all kinds of reasons. And hideously helpless. Then her heart lurched as the engine died and the boat grated against shingle. Now what? She kept her eyes tightly shut, playing dead as she was heaved over a burly shoulder. Her nostrils were assaulted by unwashed wool and sweat and tobacco as she was carried over what appeared to be rocks, by the way she was jolted. The rough handling had started up the throbbing in her temple again and her ankle was joining in. When I get home, Isobel promised herself bitterly—*if* I get home—I'll never leave it again.

She heard a door creak, then she was dumped on some kind of bed, pungent with the smell of wet wood and fish. She opened her eyes a crack to see a nightmare shape outlined by the moonlight shining through the small window of some kind of hut, and swallowed a scream as a huge hooded figure bent over her. He spoke to her roughly in Greek very different from Luke's, but when she stared at him in speechless horror he took her by the shoulders, obviously demanding a reply.

Isobel cleared her throat. 'I—I'm British. I don't understand Greek.'

This was seriously bad news to him by the stream of what

were obviously curses as he yanked her upright until her bound ankles hung over the bunk. He'd wrapped her in some kind of rug before trussing her up, which made it hard to keep her balance.

'Do you speak English?' she asked hopefully.

A negative grunt was the only response.

'Could you possibly untie my hands?' she asked without much hope. 'My wrists and shoulders are hurting.'

To her surprise, he did as she asked, then removed the rug and retied her wrists in front of her. Isobel forced herself to sit as upright as possible, horribly conscious now of how little she was wearing on her top half as he lit a lantern suspended from a hook on a roof beam. As the light fell on her the man cursed again, his eyes glaring through the slits of the hood. Isobel backed away in terror, her skin crawling as he ran his fingers through her tousled curls to frame her face. What was he going to do? Then she found out. He pushed a newspaper between her tied hands and took photographs of her with his phone, and for a finale took her breath away by flicking a knife open to slice off a lock of hair. Determined not to show fear, she glared at him defiantly as he pointed to a box which held a package and bottles of water. He fetched a metal bucket and placed it at the end of the bunk, then turned out the lamp and left the hut. The door slammed shut behind him and bolts rammed home, and shortly afterwards the outboard motor roared into action as the boat took off, leaving Isobel limp with relief because rape had not been part of the plan. Not yet, anyway.

As the moonlight faded, instead of the total darkness she'd dreaded, the first faint light of dawn took its place. Isobel's spirits rose as the light gradually increased enough for a look round her prison. She was in some kind of fisherman's hut, and a primitive one at that. The bunk was the only seating, and the mattress was damp and smelly.

The man had tied her wrists more loosely than before, which was good news. Otherwise, using the bucket would have been tricky, so would the eating and drinking part. How long was the man intending to leave her here? And who would be the lucky recipient of the hair and the candid camera shots? Luke? The kidnapper now knew she was British and obviously not some relative of Lukas Andreadis, so was he banking on the fact that she was his lover and worth ransoming? But in most cases kidnappers tended to get rid of their victims, whether the money was paid or not, didn't they? Isobel batted that thought away and set about solving more immediate problems. She had to get her hands free as the first step to getting herself out of here. There was no way she was just going to curl up in misery like a victim and wait for rescue or rape, whichever came first.

Fired with new determination, she tested the ropes. She'd deliberately tensed her wrists as the man retied them to gain a little leeway, and once she could see clearly she began tugging at the knots with her teeth. Ignoring the oily taste of the hemp, Isobel kept at it until the knot loosened and her teeth ached, but with freedom in sight she worked frantically, ignoring the soreness of her wrists until after what seemed like hours the knot finally gave and the rope fell away. Bingo! Triumphant, she smoothed her sore wrists for a while as she took a breather, then after some wriggling swung her feet up on to the bench to get to work on the ankle restraints. By some miracle, the support bandage was still in place though the ankle was aching. But with two hands instead of teeth for tools, unravelling this set of knots was marginally easier. After an endless, muscle-straining interval she managed to free herself and collapsed back on the bunk, panting but jubilant, as the ropes fell away.

The morning sun was revealing her primitive surroundings in all their glory now she had attention to spare for them. Isobel smiled sardonically as she reviewed her dramatic change of circumstances. Just a short time before she had been enjoying the luxury of Luke's villa, waited on hand and foot and coaxed to eat. Today, she was in a rude hut odorous with fishing tackle and nets, with only herself to rely on and her own two feet to get her anywhere. And, in spite of fright and the oily rope she'd been gnawing on, she was hungry. Wishing she'd eaten more last night, Isobel stood up gingerly and limped over the dank plank floor, the ankle hurting enough without her crutch to make her sweat as she grabbed her supplies. The bag contained bread, a chunk of hard cheese, a container of the inevitable olives and a few tomatoes. Panting as she got back to the bunk, Isobel eyed her haul thoughtfully. Exactly how long was the food, what there was of it, intended to last?

She ate some bread and a tomato, gnawed on a bit of the cheese, then packed the rest away for later. She drank the water thirstily, but stopped after a few needy mouthfuls. Who knew how long that had to last, either? Tired after her labours, Isobel decided a rest was only practical to sharpen her wits, and fell into such an exhausted sleep she woke to find more than an hour had gone by. Furious about taking a nap instead of looking for an escape route, it was some consolation to find she at least felt better for the rest. But now it was time to take action. She was heartily sick of being victimised by a man purely because he was bigger and stronger, like her kidnapper. And Gavin.

Isobel knelt up on the bunk to look out of the window. The

hut was in a narrow cove with rock formations and shingle edged by pines and shrubs, but hemmed in by cliffs so steep and sheer it was a dark, forbidding place. She limped over to inspect the door, which was made of solid wood planking. The memory of bolts going home confirmed that there was no possibility of opening it, so she returned to the bunk and sat down, determined to stay positive at all costs. Cheering herself on with the prospect of Joanna's reaction when she got home to describe her adventures, she reminded herself that this was a fisherman's hut. Its owner might return and help her. She rolled her eyes. In fiction, maybe. But this was reality. The only one around to give her a helping hand was herself.

Isobel leaned her forehead against the glass, then moved back, eyes narrowed. The window was small, but if she smashed the glass she might just about wriggle through. But first she had to break the window. Isobel inspected the fishing paraphernalia stacked against the wall. Nothing there to break glass. Back at the dirty window, she used a corner of the rug to wipe a section of window clear to survey her section of the beach. And made an exciting discovery. The windowpane was made of hard, opaque plastic, not glass, which was why she could barely see through it. Her eyes lit up. If she heaved the metal bucket at the window it should do the trick. She gave a hysterical little chuckle. It was a good thing she'd thought of it now, before using the bucket for its intended purpose. Steadying herself on her good foot, Isobel picked up the bucket, stood back and heaved it at the window with skill retained from her netball-playing days in school. She checked the result. The window showed a few cracks but remained disappointingly intact. Damn!

Isobel drank a little more water, then resumed her window battering. It was tiring, noisy work, but she kept on doggedly until her entire body ached with effort. Then at last she gave a yell of triumph as the window gave and shards of plastic showered outside. Covered in sweat, her breath heaving through her chest, she wrapped her hand in the rug to hammer out the remaining bits, then shook more fragments out of the rug and sat down, head bowed and hands on knees while she heaved air into her lungs. After a minute or two she straightened to assess her escape hatch. It would be a tight fit, but she would manage. No choice. She had to. And her provisions had to go with her. She knotted up the bag of food and bottles of water in the rug and scrambled up on the bunk, wincing as her ankle protested. Stop that, she ordered. Cooperate. I've got to get myself out of here. She hoisted up her makeshift bundle and lowered it outside, then let it go the short distance to the ground, praying that the bottles wouldn't burst on impact, but, to her relief, the bundle touched down quietly on the sand between the rocks.

Isobel took a deep breath, then began to wriggle her way backwards through the opening. When she was halfway out she managed to get her good leg free, tearing her leggings in the process, then clung to the window frame, breaking a fingernail as she manoeuvred the other leg out. She hung there for a moment, gasping, then let go and landed on her bottom and fell flat on her back in the sand. Good. She stayed there, panting, pleased to find she was still in one piece. Isobel sat up and slowly got to her knees, and then to her feet. Her ankle was doing its usual throbbing thing but the rest of her was in reasonable working order. She could stand if she put most of her weight on the good foot.

Isobel stood on it to lean against the wall of the hut and size up the situation. If she hung about here, hoping to catch the attention of a passing fisherman, she was far more likely to attract the attention of the kidnapper, who was bound to return sooner or later, either to exchange her for money, or… She blanked out the alternative and concentrated on a survey of the beach and the belt of greenery edging it. Beyond it, the cliffs rose even more steeply than those leading to the Villa Medusa, but her eyes lit up as she realised that what looked like a ribbon winding up the cliff was actually a path leading from the far side of the beach. It looked more user-friendly for a mountain goat than a human, but even if she climbed up it on her hands and knees she had to try rather than stay here like a sitting duck.

Isobel picked up her unwieldy bundle and, with the help of a sharp pebble, made a jagged tear in the cloth and ripped the thin rug in two. She tied one half round her shoulders for protection like a shawl, finished off the half empty bottle of water, then tied up the remaining two with the food and fastened the ends of the rug round her waist. She limped across the sand as far as she could go, then picked her way over the shingle, glad to leave the scorching sun for the shade of the pines. She winced as needles caught in her socks. Shoes would have been nice. So would a hat and sunglasses. But when she finally reached the foot of it the path was a crushing disappointment; far narrower than she'd thought, and so vertiginously steep she had no hope of climbing up it, hands and knees or any other way. She regrouped. Time to do some serious thinking. Thankful that her watch had survived intact, Isobel saw it was later than she'd realised. It had taken her far too long to get free of the ropes, and the nap had been a big mistake.

She stiffened suddenly, her heart in her throat as she heard an engine out to sea. Panting in panic, she dropped to the ground, dispensing with her bundle to wriggle under cover as the sound grew louder, and scrabbled around until she found a tree branch sturdy enough for a weapon. Just in case. She fought to lie still, ignoring the spiny plant pricking at her as the engine noise grew louder, then had a sudden change of heart. No more victim nonsense, Isobel! She scrambled to her feet, squaring her shoulders as she brandished her weapon. If it was the kidnapper she'd face him on her own two feet and put up a fight, rather than burrow into the ground like a coward. Her heart began pounding like a trip hammer as the boat came nearer; then, to her overwhelming relief, a familiar voice shouted her name and Luke leapt from the boat as it reached the shingle.

With a cry of joy Isobel dropped her weapon as he came racing towards her; the most beautiful sight she'd ever seen in her life, villainous black eye included. He swept her up in his arms, hugging her hard enough to crack her ribs as Spiro came hurrying to wring her hand in passionate relief before excusing himself to ring Eleni with the wonderful news.

'Are you hurt, Isobel?' demanded Luke roughly, slackening his hold to look her up and down.

'Not really,' she gasped. 'Please! Can we just get away before he comes back?'

'Just one man?' demanded Luke as he carried her to the *Athena*.

'Yes.'

'Can you describe him?'

Isobel shook her head. 'It was dark and he wore a hood. But he was very big, and spoke Greek with an accent very different from yours.'

'He was definitely strong,' said Luke grimly. 'He carried you down the cliff path to the beach to get to the boat. And I have made sure that path is difficult to discourage trespassers.'

She smiled valiantly. 'Good thing I was unconscious for that part!'

Luke deposited his burden very gently on a seat in the boat and, ignoring her protests that she was hot, wrapped her in a light rug very different from the one provided by the kidnapper. Luke gave her wonderfully cold water to drink and then held her close as Spiro untied the boat and jumped aboard to restart the engine. Something unclenched inside Isobel as the boat headed out into the sea and she leaned against Luke in the cool salt breeze of their passage, savouring his warmth and strength, hardly daring to believe she was safe.

'The hut was locked,' he said hoarsely, holding her close. 'You actually climbed out through that window?'

'With enormous difficulty, yes. I had to break it first.' Isobel gave him a brief account of her labours, and her idea of climbing up the cliff to escape. 'But the path was too narrow and steep, and my ankle hurt,' she finished. 'My wrists, too,' she added, and Luke swore volubly as he examined them. 'How did you know where to find me?'

'When I was young I spent half my life on these waters.' He hugged her closer. 'When the photograph came through to me from my people in Athens I was mad with worry. But once I calmed down I realised I recognised the hut, even though it is many years since I worked for the old fisherman who owned it. There are probably countless others like it but, thank the gods, I was right about this one.' His voice roughened. 'Tell me the truth, Isobel. Did this animal hurt you?'

She shook her head, knowing he meant far more than just the marks on her wrists. 'No. He put a cloth over my face with something like chloroform on it, and trussed me up. And in the hut he cut off some of my hair—did you receive that, by the way?'

'Not personally,' he said, in a tone which sent shivers down her spine. 'I was already on my way back to Chyros after Spiro rang in a frenzy to report that you were missing.'

Isobel smiled comfortingly at Spiro as he shook his head in mute remorse. 'The man left food and water with me, so I suppose he was going to come back at some point. Did he ask for money?'

'Yes. I have until ten tomorrow night to pay. My people in Athens relayed the message.' He drew in a deep, unsteady breath. 'Spiro heard something in the night and went out into the garden to investigate, but could see nothing in the darkness. Then he heard a boat start up in the cove below and went to check on you. The doors to your room had been forced and you were gone. So was the intruder, or Spiro would have been a casualty, too,' said Luke grimly.

'Thank God he didn't run into him! The man would make two of him.' Isobel shuddered at the thought.

'Even so, Spiro is deeply ashamed that he failed to keep you safe.' Luke's arms tightened. 'So am I.'

Isobel shook her head firmly. 'It's no one's fault. I'm all right. Really. Where was this place, by the way?'

'A small, uninhabited island just a short distance to the south of Chyros. Probably chosen so he could get you there quickly without being seen.'

'*Uninhabited?*' She rolled her eyes. 'So if, by some miracle, I *had* managed to climb that path up the cliff, it would have been for nothing?'

Luke nodded grimly. 'No beach on the other side, just rocks. Old Petros was a loner and spent a lot of time there. He kept a goat or two at one time, hence the path. But fishing was his main pastime. He used to bring his catch in to Chyros to sell to the tavernas, which is how I met him. He liked me, for some reason, and gave me a job in the school holidays. I was often there on the island, sharing food with him in that hut, which is why I recognised it from the photograph.' His arm tightened painfully. 'Otherwise—'

'Let's not think of otherwise,' said Isobel firmly, then sighed with relief as a familiar smudge appeared on the horizon. 'Chyros!'

CHAPTER EIGHT

To Isobel's surprise, Spiro kept well out to sea instead of making for the familiar harbour. Luke smiled at her in reassurance and held a finger to his lips as he pulled the rug up to cover her head when Spiro finally steered the *Athena* into a narrow, steep-sided cove on the far side of Chyros. He secured the boat close to the waiting Cherokee on the jetty, and jumped out to hold the Jeep's passenger door wide as Luke stepped on to the jetty with his tightly wrapped burden.

'Forgive me; I must do this,' Luke whispered as he laid Isobel on the floor between the front and back seats. 'I cannot risk someone seeing you. Just a few minutes more, and you will be safe.'

Isobel had to concentrate hard on keeping still in her wrappings as Luke drove at breakneck pace up a steep helter-skelter of a road. She relaxed a little as the Jeep eventually stopped climbing and began to descend, and when it finally turned down the drive to the villa she heaved a heartfelt sigh of relief. The instant it came to a halt Luke plucked her out to carry her inside the house, where Eleni, hysterical with relief, hurried behind as he bore Isobel upstairs to the guest room on the upper floor.

Luke unwound the rug and set her down in the big chair in

the familiar, beautiful bedroom, then stood back to look at her over Eleni's head as the little woman knelt to grasp Isobel's hands, pouring out remorse and apologies it was hard to understand with only one word in five in English.

'I'm all *right*, honestly, Eleni,' Isobel assured her unsteadily. 'Just dirty and thirsty. I'd kill for some tea.'

Luke spoke kindly to the woman in her own language and she got to her feet, scrubbing her face with the corner of her apron.

'*Me synchoreite!* I get tea.'

Luke turned to Spiro. 'Be careful, *ne*? If someone rings or calls here, we failed to find our guest.'

Spiro nodded grimly and led his wife from the room.

'Did the police get involved?' asked Isobel, eyeing the dressing on Luke's arm.

'When Spiro rang I contacted them in Athens.' Luke looked down at her with an intensity which made Isobel suddenly conscious of her sweat-stained clinging vest and torn leggings. 'Now, tell me how you feel. Truthfully.'

'As I told Eleni, I'm dirty and thirsty and my ankle hurts a bit, but I'm not too bad, all things considered.' She held out her chafed wrists. 'Do you have anything I can put on these after I shower?'

Luke's mouth twisted as he raised her hands to his lips. 'Isobel, this is all my fault. The man orchestrating this campaign thinks I will pay whatever he wants to get you back.' He looked up into her eyes. 'He is right. But I would give much to lay my hands on the scum who put you through this. And I cannot even call Dr Riga out to you yet for fear that word gets out that I have you.'

'I don't need Dr Riga,' said Isobel firmly. 'And you look battered enough already, so keep well away from the man who kidnapped me. He's a big brute.'

'Are you sure he didn't hurt you?' demanded Luke fiercely.

'Yes, though when he carried me to the hut he wasn't exactly gentle.' Her eyes flashed. 'And he went raving mad when he saw my hair.'

To her surprise, Luke looked uncomfortable. 'It was the colour. He was expecting dark hair.'

'What?' Her eyes narrowed. 'He thought he was kidnapping someone else?'

'Yes. A friend of mine. Granddaughter of the industrialist Denis Stratos—who received a ransom note this morning, also.'

All this had happened due to mistaken identity? Isobel felt a sudden violent urge to hit someone. 'No wonder the man was furious. Could you ask Eleni to fetch some clothes up here for me, please? I'm utterly desperate to get clean.'

'All your belongings are back in this room again,' he said quickly. 'You sleep here tonight and every other night, where I can keep you safe.'

'But once the kidnapper's caught it won't matter where I sleep; I can go back to the Kalypso,' said Isobel, though secretly she was not at all keen on the prospect after her adventure.

'No,' said Luke flatly. 'Until your flight to the UK, you remain here. I have rescued you twice. A third time you might not be so lucky.'

She glared at him. 'It was hardly my intention to trouble you, either time.'

'I know; I put that badly—' He broke off as Eleni came in with the tea. 'You must drink your tea in here, not on the veranda. With a telescopic lens someone could see you.'

Wonderful. 'Whatever you say,' she said wearily, utterly shattered now her adrenaline rush had receded.

'I shall leave you for a while,' said Luke, eyeing her narrowly. 'Are you really all right, Isobel? You look exhausted.'

'Hardly surprising, after my labours.' She smiled doggedly as Eleni poured tea. 'A cup of tea and a long hot shower and I'll be fine.'

Once Luke had gone, Isobel sagged in the chair, tears suddenly streaming down her face, and Eleni went on her knees beside her, rocking her in her arms as she made comforting noises. But after a while the little woman pulled away, her eyes fierce as she examined the rope marks on Isobel's wrists.

'The pig did this?'

Isobel nodded dumbly.

'Tell truth. That all?'

'Yes. Nothing worse.' Isobel gulped and scrubbed at her eyes with the tissue Eleni handed her. 'Stupid to cry now I'm safe.'

'Is natural! Now, drink tea, then shower. Want help?'

'No, I can manage.' Isobel hugged her hard. 'Oh, God, Eleni, I was so terrified that you and Spiro had been hurt.'

At which point the woman's English deserted her and she rocked Isobel in her arms again for a while before letting her go.

When Isobel finally stood under the spray, wincing as it caught her various scrapes and bruises, her mood was a long way short of the elation it should have been. She had expected Luke to make rather more fuss of her. They'd agreed to be friends, after all, so a comforting cuddle or two would have been nice. But once the first violence of his relief had abated he seemed to have switched off. And tonight she couldn't even eat with him. The terrace was as public as her bedroom veranda.

Isobel had to work hard to get her damp hair in shape with a chunk of it missing at one side. Her first priority would obviously be a haircut once she got home. She smiled wryly. How wonderfully tame life would be back at the gallery. She fought down a sudden wave of homesickness at the thought of it and went to work on her face, then covered her array of bruises with a white long-sleeved shirt and soft blue cotton jeans. But went barefoot rather than subject her tender feet to shoes. And she felt vulnerable without the ankle support, which had been so filthy she'd had to bin it. When she left the bathroom Eleni was patting the pillows invitingly on the bed, but Isobel shook her head, smiling.

'I'll just sit in this lovely comfortable chair and read.'

It seemed like hours before Luke, with a perfunctory knock on the open door, came in carrying the crutch. He was obviously fresh from a shower, with a clean dressing on his arm.

'You look better, Isobel,' he said in approval. He propped the crutch at the foot of the bed and drew up a chair.

'Cleaner, certainly. You were a very long time,' she added, then regretted it when his eyes gleamed.

'You missed me?'

'I thought you might want to know more about my miraculous escape,' she said tartly.

'I do. Every last detail. But first I had to drive down to the boat. I took the *Athena* over to the harbour while Spiro drove the Cherokee back up the hill and then down to the town to meet me in full view of the public as I docked. The object,' he added patiently, as though explaining to a child, 'was to give the impression that you were still missing.'

She flushed. 'Oh. I see.'

'As soon as I docked, Alyssa came running from the taverna to demand news,' he went on. 'I clasped her dramatically to my chest so I could whisper in her ear that you were safe, and ordered her to keep it totally secret. Then I said very loudly that I had failed to find you.' He grinned suddenly. 'She began wailing and crying, and made such a scene that she collected a crowd. At this point, apparently overcome with despair at my lack of success, I joined Spiro in the Jeep and he drove me home past a sympathetic audience.'

'Wow,' said Isobel, impressed. 'I wish I'd been there. Sorry I was cross,' she added contritely.

'It is not surprising. But you missed a wonderful performance from Alyssa. I told her not to ring the house because I need all lines open, but she will be here tomorrow, whatever happens.' He took a tube from his pocket. 'Give me your hands.'

She held them out for him to squeeze cream on her rope burns. 'Thank you. That feels good.'

His eyes held hers. 'Are there any hidden injuries that need attention?'

'No. Just the odd scrape and bruise. And my feet are a bit tender. Nothing a night's rest won't put right.'

He frowned. 'You have removed your ankle support.'

'No choice. It was dirty.'

'As soon as I can I will ask Dr Riga to replace it. In the meantime, take great care as you walk, Isobel.'

'I'll be fine now you've brought the crutch,' she assured him. 'After all, I didn't even have that when I managed to get myself out of the hut and across the beach.'

'Which still amazes me.' He breathed in deeply. 'But it is my fault that such effort was necessary. You were kidnapped not just to extort money from me, but to cause me maximum pain. My one piece of luck was the location. The kidnapper was obviously a stranger; otherwise he would have taken you somewhere more remote. Have you remembered anything else about him?'

'No.' She shrugged. 'Not that I was in any condition to take much note at the time. He grunted and swore more than he actually spoke. But when he retied my hands he did it loosely enough for me to undo the knots eventually. With my teeth,' she added in distaste. 'It was horribly oily rope and tasted foul, but I won in the end.'

Luke looked down at the hands he was still holding. 'Can you imagine,' he said without expression, 'how I felt when Spiro rang me to say you were missing?'

She thought about it. 'Guilty, maybe, because your wealth was the motive for ransom? Also because kidnappers rarely let their victims live.'

Luke looked up, his eyes glittering. 'All this and more flashed through my mind. I felt such despair and frustration—and sheer rage—that I burned to kill whoever had done this.'

Isobel felt suddenly a lot better. 'Did it matter so much to you, then?'

His dark brows shot up in disbelief. 'Can you doubt it?'

Her eyes fell as she tried to think of some kind of response.

Luke smiled crookedly and released her hands. 'You find my feelings so hard to believe?'

'Other than the guilt part, yes,' she muttered. 'I'm just a passing stranger in your life.'

'I feel I know you very well, Isobel,' he said softly, his eyes hot with a look that made her own fall again.

'That's probably because the circumstances have been so unusual.'

'Holding your delectable body in my arms so much certainly accelerated the process,' he agreed with relish.

'At least you don't have to do that any more,' she retorted. 'I'm mobile now.'

His eyes fastened on hers. 'But I still want to hold you in my arms, little friend.'

Battening down a leap of response, Isobel took in a deep breath. 'Luke, next week I'm going home. So, although I'm deeply grateful to you for saving my life—'

'Twice!'

Her eyes flashed. 'Even so, I'm afraid I have nothing to—to offer in return but my grateful thanks. I may be jumping the gun again, but holiday romances are just not my thing.'

Luke got to his feet, irritatingly unperturbed. 'I will try hard to remember that, Isobel.' He looked at his watch. 'Rest now until Eleni brings your dinner. I shall be in the study, keeping in touch with my people in Athens. Is there anything you need?'

'No, thank you,' she said, subdued, and with a formal little bow he turned away.

'Luke.'

'Yes?' He turned at the door.

She smiled shakily. 'Thank you again for rescuing me. But I'm worried. What if the man makes off with the money without being caught?'

'Then he does,' he said, shrugging.

'In which case I'll owe you a lot more than mere thanks.'

'You owe me nothing,' he retorted, suddenly grim. 'You were a guest in my house. I should have taken better care of you. This, in some small way, I can remedy now.' He strode back to her and picked her up to place her against the stacked pillows on the bed, then handed the book to her. 'Read if you must, but sleep would be better.'

Isobel smiled her thanks, but she had a lump in her throat. Again. She had to kick this crying habit. Not her style, normally. But then, nothing quite so momentous as kidnapping had ever happened in her life before. What a tale she would have to tell when she got home.

Luke ran down to the study to check with his assistant in Athens. Andres, as usual, was concise and efficient, with news that the money was ready and would be left the following evening, packaged according to instructions, in the alley alongside the indicated *kafeinion*, which was already under covert surveillance by the police. There had been no communication from the kidnapper since the original statement that the goods would be returned once he had the money.

Not right, thought Luke. 'I don't like this, Andres. Something smells wrong. I want him caught. And I need to know who's behind this. Someone's after my blood, one way or another. It has to stop.'

'I agree, *kyrie*. And with police help, and our own people watching, we shall catch him and make it stop.'

'I'll be back in the morning,' said Luke decisively.

'Better you are not! You would be an obvious target.'

'All the more reason for me to return. I am the one he wants. No argument, Andres. I have to do this.'

'Then I will cover your back, *kyrie*,' said Andres promptly.

'I was counting on that,' Luke assured him. 'Ari has his team ready in support?'

'Ready and waiting. How is the lady?'

'Doing remarkably well after her ordeal. Thanks, Andres. Keep me informed.'

Luke went outside to prowl round the garden. Given the choice, he would have returned to Athens immediately, to be right at the heart of things well in advance of zero hour. Luke's fists clenched at the thought of Isobel helpless in the kidnapper's hands. His blood ran cold at the thought of what he might have done to her before killing her. Because whoever was behind all this knew that the perfect way to make him suffer was to threaten the woman they assumed was his. But a fatal mistake had been made in choosing a kidnapper. The man had taken it for granted that the guest staying in his house on Chyros was Arianna Stratos, the woman most recently linked with him.

Luke stalked restlessly through the garden. His feelings had been indescribable as the *Athena* approached that barren little island—hope and gripping fear and then overwhelming, engulfing relief as he spotted the bright gleam of hair against the undergrowth and saw Isobel, dirty and defiant, brandishing her weapon as she prepared to do battle. One look, and all his original suspicions of her had vanished, consumed in the fire of his rage at the thought of losing her, of another man touching her, or worse. Luke smiled crookedly. How polite Isobel had been, making it plain that if he was expecting anything more from his little friend than gratitude for his trouble he was out of luck.

CHAPTER NINE

ISOBEL woke to a hand patting hers gently and smiled into Eleni's hovering face. 'What time is it?' she asked.

'Dinner time.'

'Already?' Isobel yawned as she sat upright. 'You should have woken me sooner.'

'*Kyrie* Luke said leave you rest.'

'Right. Just give me a few minutes.'

'Spiro put paintings in room downstairs,' the woman informed her.

Isobel thanked her warmly. So much had happened since painting them, she'd forgotten about her watercolours. Ten minutes later, her hair and face were as good as she could make them, but her shirt was badly creased. Not that it mattered if she was eating alone. Though she would have appreciated some company after her adventure. But, as had happened in the past with other men, maybe Luke wasn't interested in her sparkling conversation if it was the only thing on offer. Isobel's thoughts skidded to a halt. Why, exactly, was she so adamant about that? After her brush with possible death, would it be so terrible to enjoy a brief love affair with a man who appealed to her on every possible level? She leaned back in the chair with a sigh. Not terrible, at all, which was the problem. A love affair with Luke might—would—be a thing of glory for a few days. And nights. But she had to think outside the box, to the time when she flew home to the real world. So she'd pushed him away, even though every instinct had been screaming at her to celebrate life by making love with the charismatic man who'd saved that life for her. Twice.

Luke suddenly appeared in the open doorway as though her thoughts had conjured him up. 'You look very serious, Isobel.'

'I was contemplating the mysteries of life,' she said lightly. 'Is there any news?'

'Only that all arrangements are in hand.' Luke drew up a chair beside her. 'My assistant is keeping me up to speed.'

'Is she super-efficient?' And probably beautiful, too, thought Isobel glumly.

'The best. Andres Stefanides has been my right-hand man since I bought my first freighter. I would trust him with my life, Isobel,' said Luke and got up, still too restless to sit. He went over to the glass doors to open them wide and brought in the veranda table. He set it in front of Isobel, then closed and locked the doors.

'Do you *really* think there's a danger he might come here again?' she asked.

'It is best to guard against the possibility.' He slammed one fist into the other in frustration. 'I will not rest until the police have him in custody and I can find out who is pulling his strings. From your description, he sounds like another hired thug, so there must be some mastermind behind him.'

She hesitated. 'It couldn't possibly be your grandfather? Because of his wife's death?'

Luke shook his head. 'Even if he did the unthinkable and hired a man to kill someone of his own blood, Theo would not have arranged the abduction. Arianna's grandfather is a lifelong friend.'

'You mean the kidnapper thought I was this Arianna?' said Isobel, eyes narrowed.

'Yes. She is a good friend of mine.'

'Pillow variety?'

'No. We share the kind of relationship you say you yearn for, Isobel. She is an intelligent, handsome woman whose company I enjoy when we get together, but—'

'But she's not the type you take to bed.'

'No.' Luke lifted an expressive shoulder. 'She is proof that it is possible for a man and woman to be just friends, Isobel.'

'I just wish more men felt the same. When I was in the hut, wondering if the man was going to come back and finish me off, I wondered if I'd ever see any of my friends again, Joanna most of all. It was an extra spur to get myself out.' Isobel smiled. 'And then you came, so all's well that ends well.'

'You should not have been forced to endure such treatment,' said Luke bitterly.

She shrugged. 'I survived. By the way, when he found he had the wrong woman, surely whoever's behind this must have wondered if you'd pay to get me back?'

'You were a guest in my house, whoever you were,' said Luke with emphasis. 'He knew I would pay. Though he made a big mistake with old Denis Stratos. Arianna was actually there in the room with her grandfather when the ransom demand arrived.'

Eleni beamed at them both as she came in to lay the table. For two, Isobel noted, brightening, as Spiro followed with a tray of steaming dishes.

Luke thanked them and smiled at Isobel as the couple left them to their dinner. 'You look surprised.'

'I am. I was expecting to dine alone tonight.'

'You would prefer that?'

Isobel shook her head irritably. 'Of course I wouldn't.'

'Then you must eat well tonight,' he urged. 'You must be very hungry, Isobel.'

'Oddly enough, I wasn't when we arrived home. I was just dirty and thirsty—' She broke off at the look he gave her. 'What is it?'

'You said "home".'

She flushed. 'I suppose the villa felt like that after my adventures.' She went on eating for a moment, then met his watchful eyes. 'In the hut I thought I might never live to eat another meal of any kind.'

Luke's mouth twisted as he put out a hand to cover hers. 'Do not think of it any more, Isobel. I have you safe now. And I swear I will keep you that way.'

'Right. Let's talk about pleasanter things.' She raised a quizzical eyebrow. 'Tell me about this Arianna of yours.'

'She is not mine!' Luke grinned. 'Arianna is an attractive, intellectual woman who refuses to marry any of the men her family keep bringing out for her.'

'Are you one of those?'

He shook his head. 'Due to the circumstances of my birth, I am not considered eligible.'

'Even though you're the grandson of Theo Andreadis?'

'Since he refuses to acknowledge the relationship, yes.'

'Would you like him to?'

His mouth tightened. 'Would you, in the same situation?'

Isobel gave it some thought. 'If he was the only relative I had it's possible I might make some kind of move towards détente, yes.'

'I do not possess your capacity for forgiveness. Also your

experience of grandparents was very different from mine,' he reminded her.

'True.' She smiled fondly at the memory. 'I was very lucky. But tell me more about Arianna.'

'We dine together occasionally, and if she needs an escort for some function her family insists she attend, I help her out. Which is no hardship. She is good company and I am fond of her.'

'Is she fond of you?'

'Of course,' he said, grinning. 'But she is in love with someone else.'

'So why doesn't he escort her?'

Luke smiled wryly. 'Arianna is a follower of Sappho. Her lover is a woman. But, other than me, and now you, no one knows that.'

'That kind of secret must be hard to keep,' said Isobel. 'But at least she has one thing going for her—she didn't get kidnapped.'

Luke laughed and seized her hand to kiss it. 'She would have been more of a handful for the kidnapper than you, Isobel. Arianna is built on heroic lines.' He eyed her challengingly. 'So, I have told you about the woman in my life. Now tell me about the men in yours. There must have been other men in your life before the swine who tried to force you.'

She winced. 'There were several in college, of course, but the ones who remain constant in my life are Leo and Josh Carey. Their family lived near my grandparents, so we grew up together. When they were teenagers they had a party. Joanna, the new kid on the block at the time, was invited to it, and the four of us have been firm friends ever since. Jo and I had boyfriends, of course, and the twins, who are doctors now, attract women like magnets, but Jo and I have a special relationship with them. Though Jo is married now.'

'And does her husband approve of these men?'

'Of course. But it wouldn't matter to her if he didn't. Jo is fiercely loyal.'

Luke smiled. 'I think you are, too, Isobel.'

'I try to be. Besides, I've known the twins since nursery school. To me, they're like brothers.'

'Ah, but do they look on you as a sister?'

'Of course they do.' She looked at the straight-backed chair he was sitting on, legs outstretched. 'You can't be comfortable on that. If I lie on the bed you can have the easy chair. Unless you have things to do.'

'What could be more important than spending the evening with you, Isobel?' He stood up. 'But first I shall go down to the study and check again with Andres. Though there can be no real news or he would have contacted me. Then I shall come back and take advantage of your offer. Unless you need sleep?' he added.

'*No.*' She shook her head so emphatically he frowned.

'You are nervous about sleeping?'

'Not exactly. But I'd like to be a lot more tired tonight before I try.' She smiled ruefully. 'It was a bad move to sleep before dinner.'

'Rest was vitally necessary after your ordeal.' His eyes darkened as he looked down at her. 'I would give much to have spared you that.'

'But you rescued me—again,' she pointed out.

'For which I have not been suitably rewarded,' he said casually and strolled to the door, slanting a glittering smile over his shoulder. 'Is there anything you need when I come back?'

'Nothing, thank you.'

Isobel wondered what Luke meant by a suitable reward. Who was she trying to kid? What would any man expect under the circumstances? She piled the pillows against the headboard and propped herself upright against them.

When Luke came back she eyed him expectantly. 'Any news?'

'No. Just that all is in readiness for tomorrow night, and I shall leave early in the morning. I shall be there on the scene when the ransom money is claimed.'

'*What?* Are you mad?' Isobel stared at him, horrified. 'Surely it's best to leave the police to deal with that! You've already escaped a stabbing; you might not be so lucky a second time.'

His face set into lines which made argument futile. 'Then that is my fate and cannot be avoided. This is something I must do, Isobel.' He sat on the edge of the bed and took her hand. 'Surely you can understand this.'

'Oh, I do,' she said with hostility. 'It's all down to testosterone. But I don't approve.' But, if he was taking off in the morning, maybe this was a good time to give him her present, just in case… She pushed the thought away. 'I should have asked you to fetch something for me.'

'I will fetch it now. What is it?'

'The watercolours I was working on. Spiro put them safe somewhere, in the room I was using downstairs.'

Isobel felt tense as she waited for him to bring the paintings. A man like Lukas Andreadis could buy whatever expensive artwork he fancied. Would he consider her efforts amateurish? The pool painting was no Hockney, but she hoped Luke would like it as a keepsake just the same.

He came back quickly, holding a large package. 'Spiro wrapped them up very carefully,' he said, handing it to her.

'He's such a star, your Spiro,' said Isobel warmly. 'Eleni, too. You're lucky to have them.'

'I know this.' Luke gestured at the package impatiently. 'Open it.'

Isobel removed the wrapping paper carefully, then handed him the painting of the pool.

Luke stood looking down at it, his face inscrutable, and then said the last thing she expected to hear. 'So. You really do paint.'

Isobel's eyes blazed as she realised what he meant. 'My sketches didn't convince you, then. You still suspected me of wanting a story for some tabloid—or, worse still, that I was a tourist out for a holiday thrill.'

'However beautiful and appealing you were, past experience made me suspicious,' he admitted, and gave her a long, unsmiling look. 'I soon discovered that you were neither of those things.'

'But you still doubted that I could paint!'

'If I did, I doubt no longer. This is exquisite.' He was so obviously sincere she calmed down. 'You are not only an artist, but a very gifted one, Isobel. You create atmosphere. I feel both the cool of the water *and* the heat of the day in your painting.'

'It's a present for you—a very small way to thank you for all your kindness,' she said with formality.

He bowed, equally formal. '*Efcharisto poli*, Isobel. I am honoured.' He put the painting very carefully on the dressing table. 'I shall have it framed in Athens and hang it in my bedroom there.' He watched closely as she unwrapped the painting of the beach. 'This also is wonderful.'

'It's *my* keepsake. To take home to look at and convince myself that all this really happened.'

Luke took the painting to join the other one, then sat beside her on the bed. 'As I said before, Isobel, I shall need no reminders of my trespasser. But I shall treasure the painting because it is not only beautiful, but a gift from you.'

'Now you know I really am an artist!' she said acidly, then looked at him in appeal. 'I wish you wouldn't go there tomorrow, Luke.'

'You are afraid I shall be killed?'

'Of course I am!'

'I was brought up in a hard school. I can look after myself. And I am not fool enough to go there alone. Andres and my security team will be in the background in support.' Luke looked into her eyes, as though assessing her mood, then drew her into his arms and held her close. 'Do not worry, Isobel.'

'I can't help it. I'll have nightmares tonight.'

'I know a remedy for that,' he whispered.

'Cocoa?'

He let out a smothered crack of laughter. 'I tasted that once in England, but I doubt that we have any here. My remedy is even sweeter, Isobel,' he added in a tone which sent her pulse racing. 'I must go down and tell Spiro what hour I intend to leave.' He kissed her fleetingly on the lips and brushed a hand over her hair.

Isobel lay frowning at the door he'd closed behind him. Had that been a *goodnight, sleep well* kind of kiss? She slid carefully off the bed to collect the beautifully laundered nightgown Eleni had left ready and limped to the bathroom, impatient with herself. He probably thought his doubts had made her angry. Maybe normally they would have. But tomorrow he was going to risk his life to hunt down the man out for his blood. She shivered, knowing she had no hope of any sleep tonight, for more reasons than one. She should have been more blunt and simply asked Luke to sleep with her. Best cure of all for nightmares—and probably a good many other things. Surviving kidnap had put things into perspective, teaching her that life was not only short, but could also be very sweet if she let it.

Isobel went over to the veranda windows, tested them to see that they were locked securely, then returned to the bed, picked up her book and sat up against the pillows. If Luke wasn't coming back, insomnia would be her fate. But she could at least read, and leave her bedside lamp on as her candle in the dark. The story was by one of her favourite authors, but the intricate mediaeval mystery, though gripping and beautifully written, failed to hold her attention. Then her eyes flew up in surprise as Luke came in and very deliberately locked the door behind him.

'As I thought, we have no cocoa,' he said, his eyes holding hers as he walked slowly to the bed. 'So we must try my remedy instead.'

Isobel licked the tip of her tongue over suddenly dry lips. 'You didn't say, exactly, what that was.'

Luke smiled as he sat on the edge of the bed. 'It is very simple, *hriso mou*. I just hold you in my arms all night and keep you safe.'

Isobel's heart turned over. 'Sounds most effective,' she said shakily.

'It is. There is just one problem. Or possibly more than one.'

'Oh?'

'If I hold you in my arms I will not sleep.' His eyes blazed. 'But I will gladly endure insomnia to guard you from night-mares, Isobel.'

Her eyes fell. 'I seem to be constantly in your debt. How will I ever repay you?'

'I can think of a way.' Luke smoothed a hand over her hair. 'Can you?'

'Yes,' she said, burning her boats. 'Is it the same way as yours?'

Luke growled as he pulled her into his arms. 'You are tormenting me, Isobel *mou*,' he whispered, his lips a tantalising inch from hers. 'I want you. Tell me you want *me*.'

Of *course* she wanted him. At this moment she wanted him more than anything or anyone she'd ever wanted before. After all the trauma, she *deserved* this. It would be her reward equally as much as Luke's. And if things went wrong tomorrow... She shivered and Luke's arms tightened, his victorious smile hidden in her hair.

'Talk to me, *hriso mou.* You said your thanks were all you had to give. Have you changed your mind?'

'Yes,' she muttered into his chest. 'So stop talking and make love to me, Lukas Andreadis—before I change it back again.'

He let out a shout of laughter and leapt up to strip off his clothes. But as he moved naked to the bed she held up her hand.

'No. Just stand still for a moment, as you did by the pool.'

She let her eyes move slowly over the burnished bronze curls, and the eyes that glowed like coals in his taut face. She lingered over the broad shoulders, the torso that tapered into a lean waist and long muscular legs, and the stirring masculinity between them. To Isobel's delight, colour rose along his sculpted cheekbones.

'I refuse to just stand here while you look at me.'

'Why not?'

His eyes flared. 'Because my body is betraying me!'

'So I see,' said Isobel, suddenly reckless as she took her nightgown over her head and pulled the covers back for him.

Luke slid in beside her and with a groan of pleasure held her close, his hands smoothing down her back to mould every curve and hollow of her body to his. 'I have dreamed of this,' he said into the angle where her neck met her shoulder.

Isobel sighed and wriggled closer, delighting in the tremor she felt run through him. 'I refused to let myself dream of it.'

'Because you did not want to make love with me?'

'No, because I did.'

He growled in triumph and kissed her fiercely. His lips were warm and skilled and now they were naked together the first touch of them on hers sent her so dizzy with delight she surged against him. And with her breasts crushed against his chest she found his heart was pounding in unison with hers as his kisses sent her blood rushing through her veins, and her body turned into one entire erogenous zone.

He raised his head and smiled in triumphant possession. 'You are so lovely, Isobel. It is impossible to believe, now, that I was angry with you that first day on the beach.'

'You frightened the life out of me.'

He tensed. 'Are you frightened now?'

'No.' She moved closer. 'Make love to me, Luke. Make me glad to be alive!'

He obeyed with such fervour Isobel's pulse raced as the heat from his kisses ran through her like a jolt of electricity. She pressed closer, glorying in the feel of his skin against hers until he moved her away a fraction so that his lips could move down her throat in a string of soft, sweet kisses, and her breasts grew taut in anticipation as she felt the heat of his breath on her skin. He made love to each breast in turn with lips and tongue and gently grazing teeth, his caresses flooding her with hot, liquid arousal as her body filled with an urgency so new and overwhelming she shook with the force of it.

Luke stiffened. 'Do not tremble. I will stop if you wish.'

'I don't wish. Go on—*please*!' She gloried in his renewed caresses, making a little relishing sound deep in her throat as his hands moved lower to stroke the satiny curve below her waist. But she gasped as his fingers aroused turbulence with the most intimate caress of all, his mouth devouring hers with a kiss so possessive and overwhelming her blood seemed to turn to steam. He looked deep into her eyes, asking a question she answered with such an impatient little nod he smiled in triumph and surged inside her, filling her to such capacity Isobel's heart lurched with the shock of it. For a long, throbbing moment they lay utterly still, then her inner muscles clenched around him in fierce invitation and he took her with him on a surging, accelerating climb towards some fiery, longed for peak he reached at last before her, then held her tightly until her body arched against him, convulsed in throbbing waves of release.

Luke stayed still for a long, silent interval while their hearts slowed, pinning her to the bed with his weight. At last he rolled over onto his back, drawing her close against him as he smoothed the damp curls away from her forehead. 'Look at me, Isobel.'

Reluctantly, she opened heavy eyes to meet the possessive black gaze.

'Did I hurt you, *hriso mou*?' he asked softly.

'No.' Isobel heaved in a deep, unsteady breath. 'But you surprised me.'

'Surprised?' He frowned. 'Why?'

'After the episode with Gavin, I was sure I'd never want to make love again, ever.' Isobel met his eyes squarely. 'But with you it was as if we were climbing together, and I'd die if I didn't reach the summit.'

His eyes glittered in triumph. 'But you did reach it, *glykia mou, ne*?'

'Not only reached it, I soared off it in free fall!'

Luke threw back his head and laughed in unashamed male satisfaction. 'It is so good for a man to hear that.'

Isobel smiled wryly. 'You sounded very Greek just then.'

He nodded with sudden arrogance. 'Because that is what I am, and proud of it. And you are an English rose, Isobel, and so beautiful and intelligent I find it hard to believe no man has wanted to marry you.'

'One did a couple of years ago. But when he started talking about mortgages and urging me to get a proper job it put me off marriage permanently.'

Luke laughed scornfully. 'The fool wanted to make you into someone else.'

'Exactly,' said Isobel, delighted he understood. 'So we broke up.' She sighed. 'But not without a fight on his part. He wanted Isobel the woman, but not Isobel the artist.'

'I want them both,' said Luke, and flipped her over on her back to lean over her, his handsome face intent with an expression that made her pulse race. 'Forget all other men; you are mine now,' he whispered and kissed her, and Isobel wreathed her arms round his neck and drew him closer. She *was* his. For now. But now was all they had together. In a few days she would be leaving Chyros to go back to the real world, where there was no place in her life for someone like Lukas Andreadis. But that life seemed very far away and unreal as he made love to her in the hot reality of the present, taking infinite pleasure in the responses he wrung from her. His lips moved over her face and throat, then continued slowly down until she felt those crisp bronze curls against her skin as he kissed her in a place unused to such attention. His lips and tongue caressed her so skilfully they sent her climbing to a different peak of pleasure she experienced alone. And in triumph Luke held her close as she gasped in the throes of it.

CHAPTER TEN

ONCE again Isobel heard the helicopter chop away at first light, and said a swift, fierce prayer for the pilot. She slid down in the bed, intending to lie there for a moment, but when she woke again a glance at her watch catapulted her out of bed in such a hurry to snatch up her nightgown she tripped as she pulled it on and only just managed to stop from falling as Eleni came in.

'You hurt?' she demanded, coming to help.

'No, no, I'm fine. I was just in a hurry for the bathroom,' said Isobel, embarrassed. 'I want a shower before breakfast.'

'*Kyrie* Luke left early,' said the little woman glumly. 'You heard?'

'Yes.'

'How you feel today?'

'Pretty good, Eleni. I'm none the worse for my adventure.' She smiled. 'And for once I really fancy some breakfast this morning.'

Isobel raced through her shower, then eyed herself critically in the steamed up mirror, surprised to see she looked much the same as usual. What had she expected? Evidence of sin? But it had been bliss, not sin. The dreamy look in her eyes soon changed to apprehension. She hugged the towel around her, suddenly cold at the thought of Luke acting out his *High Noon* scenario later.

Determined to stay strong, no matter what happened, Isobel got dressed and did her hair and face, and limped as fast as she could into the bedroom when her phone rang.

'*Kalimera*, Isobel. How are you today?'

'Luke, are you back already? I'm ashamed to say I've slept half the morning away. But I feel good. Even my eye is back to normal.'

'Unlike mine!'

'Yours is *very* sexy.' She chuckled. 'I really go for the pirate look.'

'I am so happy to hear that. I would have given much to stay and kiss you awake this morning. But I have news, Isobel. When I arrived at my apartment I found a hand-written note among my mail giving the location of Petros's island. Like the man who attacked me, your kidnapper was probably threatened in some way, but he has a conscience, it seems, and could not leave you there to perish. Even so, be careful today. Stay close to the house.'

'Yes, Luke.'

'I so like to hear you say that. When I come home I shall ask more questions that require the same answer.'

Isobel's eyebrows rose. What did he mean by that? 'Luke, I'll be desperately worried. So ring me tonight after—afterwards.'

'I will. But do not worry, *hriso mou*. I will take no chances, I swear. Now, eat.'

Worried or not, hot rolls and butter, followed by cup after cup of coffee, tasted wonderful to Isobel. At the same time yesterday she would have sold her soul for even part of the meal. She was about to ask Eleni for more coffee when she heard a car coming down the drive and, soon afterwards, Alyssa came running from the kitchen, beaming.

'*Kalimera*, Isobel. After your ordeal you should be shattered, but you look wonderful.'

'I feel fine.' Isobel smiled warmly. 'I was just about to ask Eleni for more coffee.'

'Unnecessary, *glykia mou*. She's on her way with it right now.'

By the time Eleni left them to their coffee, Alyssa was vibrating with impatience.

'So, Isobel! Did Luke tell you about my masterly performance when he returned on the *Athena* without you?'

Isobel laughed. 'He certainly did. He said you're a terrific actress.'

'Drama queen, he means!' Alyssa grinned, flipping back a lock of shining dark hair as she struck a pose. 'I rather fancy myself as Medea. Or possibly Elektra. But never mind that. Tell me what happened—every last detail.' She sobered abruptly. 'You must have been so terrified, Isobel.'

'Oddly enough, when I woke up in the boat my first reaction was fury. But the fright soon kicked in when I found I was tied up. I hated feeling so helpless.' Isobel gulped some coffee, then told Alyssa what happened, right up to the moment Luke arrived in the *Athena* to rescue her.

'For the second time!' Alyssa's lips curved in a wicked little smile. 'I trust you rewarded him generously?'

'Absolutely,' said Isobel, returning the smile in kind. 'I gave him the watercolour I painted.'

Alyssa rolled her eyes. 'Surely you can think of something more exciting than a painting?'

'Luke liked it.' Isobel's smile faded. 'I hope it will remind him of me after I leave.'

Alyssa snorted. 'He will never forget *you*, Isobel!'

'You're probably right. I've been nothing but trouble to him from the moment we met.'

'I doubt that. What man thinks of a gorgeous blonde as trouble?'

Isobel coloured. 'Luke told me he likes his women dark and curvy.'

'He has changed his mind since he met you, *glykia mou*.'

'What does that mean?'

'My sweet, more or less. Does Luke say that?'

'We're not on those kind of terms.'

'If you stayed, you soon would be,' said Alyssa firmly. 'So stay. Please. I would love you to come to my wedding.'

Isobel smiled wistfully. 'I would love it, too, but I must get back to my job. I've used up all my holiday allowance for this year.'

Alyssa sighed, then rummaged in her bag and handed over a card. 'These are my telephone numbers. Ring me if you change your mind.'

'I will.' Isobel smiled warmly. 'Thanks for coming to see me.'

'Nothing could have kept me away! It amazes me that you survived such a horrible experience so bravely. Me, I would have nightmares.' Alyssa touched the uneven lock of hair over Isobel's ear, then glanced at her watch with regret. 'I must go. Since Luke is away, why not come down to the taverna tonight? I could fetch you, and my parents would love to meet you.'

Isobel was touched. 'It's a lovely thought, Alyssa, but I'm not quite up for that right now and I'm not sure I should be seen yet. Can I take a rain check?'

'Of course. Ring me if you need me. Any time. Take care.' She kissed Isobel's cheek, then rushed off to talk to Eleni on her way out and a moment later her car roared away up the cypress-lined drive, leaving Isobel feeling restless and on edge, and wondering what to do with the rest of her day.

After trying to read for a while, Isobel gave up and got out her drawing materials. As a change from watercolours she would try a pencil portrait of Luke. Portraits were not normally her area of expertise, but the forceful, handsome features of Luke took shape on her drawing pad with such ease and speed that by late afternoon Isobel had achieved a strikingly accurate likeness. When Eleni was allowed to see the finished sketch she called Spiro to marvel at Isobel's skill, and it was so obvious that both of them lusted after the drawing Isobel promised to do another to keep herself occupied as she wondered what was happening to Luke.

At that particular moment Luke was in his office, in a meeting with Andres and various members of his staff and security force, all of whom were arguing that one of them should take his place at the designated ransom drop, a *kafeinion* in the Psyrri district of Athens.

Luke heard them out until the hubbub showed signs of abating, then held up his hand. 'I appreciate your offers, but this is personal for me. To wreak vengeance on me, this man has caused harm to a lady who is a visitor to our country, also a guest in my house. Therefore, gentlemen, I must confront this man myself before I hand him over to the police. Who,' he added, 'agreed to my keeping out of sight until the man actually tries to take the money.'

'But the criminal knows you,' said Ari Constantinou, Luke's massive head of security. 'You've survived a stabbing already, *kyrie*. You might not be so lucky a second time.'

'The intention was never to have me killed. To get the

money, he needs me alive.' Luke's eyes hardened. 'But he made a big mistake in kidnapping a lady under my protection.'

There were loud exclamations of assent from everyone present.

'So this is the plan I have worked out with Ari,' said Andres, after a nod from Luke. 'I shall go early and drink coffee at a table by the window looking out on the alley. Two of you will occupy another near the door. Another will keep watch from the men's room which overlooks the back of the alley. The boss will keep out of sight until nearer the time, and the rest of the team will be with Ari in the bar opposite. The police surveillance team will stay out of sight as *kyrie* Andreadis requested.'

'They were happy with this arrangement?' asked a voice.

'No,' said Luke. 'They wanted me to keep well away.' He smiled grimly. 'I refused.'

Later, in the stiflingly hot night, obeying an instinct that prodded him like a goad, Luke was an hour early when he began strolling amongst Athenian café society in the warren of streets that comprised the Psyrri district. He made for the designated *kafeinion* and paused on the corner opposite, smiling a greeting at one of his security men, who took his cue like a casual bystander enjoying a chat while they kept secret watch on the alley.

'You are early, *kyrie*,' said the man softly, then swore violently as a fire alarm blared in the *kafeinion*, sending everyone streaming out into the street. Luke shot through the scattering throng into the alley and launched himself in a flying tackle to ground a big, burly figure about to snatch the ransom bag. Luke fought to keep the man on the ground until help arrived, and in seconds Luke's security team closed in on them and the man was pulled to his feet to face the police, eyes rolling in fear as he was secured and hustled into the police van now blocking the alley.

'I was allowed to observe while he was being questioned later,' Luke told Isobel when he rang for the second time to give details. 'Once in custody, the man begged protection for his family against Zena and Zoe Karras, twin sisters of the dead Melina Andreadis. As I suspected, they were the driving force behind this all along. Just like the man who attacked me, your kidnapper's wife and children had been threatened by the two harpies. But he swore he was no killer, which is why he sent me the note giving me your location.'

'And he never actually hurt me,' added Isobel.

'But he tied you up and left you in that hut,' said Luke grimly, then continued to tell her that the police went straight to the Karras house to question the sisters, who promptly went berserk with fury at the failure of their plan and poured everything out in a flood of venom against him, which shocked even the battle-hardened detectives. Luke laughed cynically. 'But the sisters' vendetta against me was more for the loss of the generous allowance Melina had made them, than for her death. I was informed later that they blamed me for her death and everything else wrong in their lives.'

'They meant to have you killed?'

'No. Just to wound and harm me in any way possible, out of pure venom. As a source of money, I was no good to them dead.'

Isobel shivered, her knuckles white on the phone. 'What was to happen to me?'

'They were too hysterical to make any sense by the time they were taken into custody, but Andres is related to one of the policemen interrogating them, so I shall know more eventually.' His voice dropped a tone. 'But, no matter what they intended, you are safe now, *hriso mou*. You can sleep tonight.'

'I'll probably have nightmares!'

'If I were there with you I could provide a cure for those,' he said softly.

The mere thought of it made her weak at the knees. 'When will you be back?'

'As soon as I can, Isobel. I must work with Andres for a while first today. Even without all this drama I have been neglecting my business interests since you came into my life, Miss Isobel James!'

'So sorry about that. Never mind. I'll soon be gone.'

'I know this very well,' he assured her darkly. 'When I get back we will spend every possible moment together before you leave.'

Isobel put her phone on the bedside table, limp with relief now it was all over and Luke was safe. But she was very thoughtful as she settled into the pillows. If Luke intended to spend every moment possible with her before she left, did he mean in as well as out of bed? And, if so, what would Eleni and Spiro think of the arrangement? Isobel bit her lip. She had become so fond of the couple the thought of losing their respect was painful. She hugged a pillow to her chest fiercely. If she'd known beforehand that she'd be in danger of falling madly in love during her holiday she would have steered clear of these magical Greek islands. The holiday had been intended as a recovery programme, both from working overtime for weeks and from the hateful episode with Gavin. But now she would need all the hard work she could get once she was home to help her recover from her Greek odyssey. And from Luke. She sighed. If she wasn't her sparkling self for a while, at least Jo would assume that her hair-raising adventures were the reason. Whereas the real problem would be that she was pining for the man who'd rescued her from them.

The next day seemed endless. Luke rang twice in snatched moments between meetings, but he was too busy for more than a word or two. And when Alyssa rang later she apologised because the taverna was short-staffed and she had to work all day rather than drive up to the Villa Medusa as she'd intended. To occupy herself, Isobel finished the drawing of Luke for Eleni and Spiro, ate the lunch put in front of her and in between took walks in the garden with her stick at regular intervals to exercise her ankle and pass the time until Luke got back. After that, her time with him would be so brief she was determined to make the most of every minute—once he tore himself away from his empire to fly back to Chyros.

When Eleni apologised because dinner would be served an hour later that evening Isobel assured her it was fine with her and went carefully up the stairs, supporting herself on the carved banister rail as she went. In preparation for Luke's return tomorrow she would use the hour for the kind of top-to-toe beauty treatment she rarely had time, or inclination, for at home.

Isobel was sitting on the veranda as the sun set, waving her newly painted toes around to dry the polish, when her heart leapt at the sound she hadn't been expecting until the next day. Tense with excitement, she leaned out over the balcony rail as Luke's helicopter circled round to land, then forced herself to wait for him to come to her. She went barefoot into the bedroom, listening to the sound of greetings downstairs as Luke brought Spiro up to date, her pulse racing in time with his footsteps as Luke ran upstairs, and at last he was there in

the doorway, arms outstretched. She flew into them and he
buried his face in the fragrant mass of her newly washed hair,
holding her close against his thudding heart.

Luke raised his head at last, smiling down into her eyes.
'*Kalispera*, Isobel.'

'Hi,' she said, smiling radiantly. 'You forgot to tell me you
were coming home today.'

'I did not forget. I wanted to surprise you.'

She wagged a finger. 'But you let Spiro know, because
Eleni asked to put dinner later tonight. She never said a word.'

'On my orders,' Luke said, and put her away from him to
look down into her eyes. 'I wanted to see your face when I
arrived, and now I have seen it and know you are glad to see
me I want to kiss you very badly. But if I do I might not stop,
and I need time to make myself worthy of my beautiful dinner
companion.'

'Thank you, kind sir. I'll wait for you on the terrace.'

'Wait up here and I shall carry you down,' he said promptly,
but she shook her head.

'With care, I can manage without my crutch now if I go
barefoot and carry these to put on downstairs.' Isobel grinned
at him as she picked up her sandals. 'Don't be long. I'm hungry.'

Isobel had felt no enthusiasm for dining alone, but with Luke
for such unexpected company she did full justice to the celebration meal Eleni and Spiro took such pleasure in serving
them, both of them blazingly happy now that the man they
loved like a son had faced down his enemies and returned to
them safely.

At intervals Luke left the table to answer the phone to well
wishers who had seen the news, among them Alyssa
Nicolaides, who apologised for disturbing him but had been

instructed to convey her parents' relief, along with hers, that he had survived yet another dangerous encounter unscathed.

'The gods must be watching over you, Lukas *mou*. Give my love to Isobel,' Alyssa added sweetly as she said goodbye.

'That was Alyssa,' said Luke as he resumed his place at the table. 'She sent you her love. I shall leave all other calls to the machine. If there is anything urgent from Andres he will use my private line.' He yawned hugely. 'Forgive me, Isobel, I had very little sleep last night.'

'I'm not surprised.' She abandoned the pomegranate she'd been toying with. 'Do you want to go to bed?'

Luke jumped up to pull out her chair. 'Zeus, yes, I do. I will tell Spiro he can lock up.'

'Thank Eleni for a wonderful dinner, Luke, but don't be long,' said Isobel, then flushed hectically at the look her gave her.

As Luke strode off towards the kitchen Isobel slipped off the sandals and began her usual careful ascent of the stairs but, before she was even halfway up, he caught up with her and carried her the rest of the way and along the landing to her room. Once inside, he kicked the door shut and laid her on the bed, then cast himself down beside her and took her in his arms, his face buried against her neck.

'Last night,' he said, his breath hot against her skin, 'I thought of this when I was watching that alley, waiting to seize the man who had kidnapped you.'

'I thought of it every minute of the day,' she admitted huskily. 'Then you rang me to say you were safe, and I could breathe again.'

Luke raised his head to look in her eyes. 'You cared that much?'

'Yes.' She wriggled closer. 'Now tell me about it again. Was it a shock to learn the Karras sisters were behind the vendetta?'

'No. After their behaviour towards me at Melina's funeral it was no surprise at all.' Luke kissed her with sudden heat. 'Now forget them, *agapi mou*, and concentrate on me.'

Isobel woke alone the next morning and had showered and dressed before Luke came to find her.

'*Kalimera,*' he said, taking her in his arms.

'Good morning.' She smiled up at him. 'How are you today?'

'Now there is no longer danger to you, I feel as though a great weight has rolled from my shoulders, Isobel. I also feel hungry,' he added, and kissed her. 'For breakfast also, you understand. And while we eat you shall tell me what you would like to do today.'

They had reached the coffee stage when Isobel made her request. 'I'd love a swim.' She laid a hand on his, smiling at him cajolingly. 'You're here now, so you can hardly refuse me a second time.'

Luke raised the hand to his lips. 'Of course you can swim. Milos is not here today so this is a good time.'

Isobel eyed him narrowly. 'Is Milos the reason why you wouldn't let me use the pool before?'

'Yes,' he said bluntly. 'I had seen what you wear to swim, remember.'

'My bikini is perfectly respectable,' she retorted.

He snorted. 'When I first saw you on my beach I thought you were naked.'

'Only because the bikini's pink—at least it was.' She made a face. 'Not that I'll ever wear it again.'

After breakfast they went upstairs together, Luke's arm in support after an argument about carrying her.

'Give me ten minutes,' she said at her bedroom door, then hurried to change into a sleek gentian-blue swimsuit; her only alternative to the bikini. Isobel eyed the various bruises which had now matured into multicoloured glory, then shrugged philosophically. Luke had seen them all before. She put a filmy tunic on top, collected a bath towel and opened the door to Luke. 'That was a lot less than ten minutes.'

'Why waste time apart?' said Luke and bent to pick her up, but Isobel shook her head.

'If you just hold my hand I'll manage the stairs perfectly well.'

'No matter. I need to hold you in my arms. Indulge me, *ne*?'

Luke set her down on one of the reclining chairs at the pool's edge, then took off the T-shirt and jeans he was wearing over his swimming gear. 'Shall I help you take off this pretty thing?' he asked, eyeing the tunic.

'That I can do myself!' She slipped the garment over her head and stood up unaided.

His eyes narrowed to a hot gleam as they moved over her. 'That is even more alluring than the bikini!'

'I thought you'd be pleased that I'm more covered up,' she said primly, and he laughed and scooped her up to run along the pool, ignoring her frantic protests as he jumped in the water with her.

Spluttering and laughing as she surfaced, Isobel pushed him away, then took off down the pool in the stylish crawl which had won races in school. But Luke followed her with the grace and power she'd so much admired from her balcony and passed her easily, thrusting his wet curls back as he waited at the end for her. She gave him a challenging grin as she did a racing turn and swam off again, and with a shout he gave chase to swim beside her for a few lengths. When Isobel called it quits he hoisted himself out of the pool and lifted her out to wrap her in a towel.

'You are like a mermaid in the water, Isobel. Do you want to go in, or will you wait for me while I finish my swim?'

'I'll sit here in the sun for a minute or two,' she panted. 'I'm out of condition. I haven't done this for a while. Besides, I want to watch you.'

Luke gave her a quick kiss and dived into the pool. Isobel watched, transfixed, for once wishing she had a camera to preserve the moment as he powered through the water for several lengths of the pool. At last he swung himself up beside her, breathing hard.

'I think you should go in now, Isobel.' He startled her by casually stripping off to towel himself down before pulling on his jeans. He handed the filmy tunic over and bent to pick her up.

'You can't feel like carrying me after all that exercise,' she said severely, but Luke merely chuckled and carried on through the hall, not even out of breath, she saw, impressed, as Eleni came hurrying to offer coffee. He nodded and gave instructions in her own language as he carried on up the stairs.

'I said to give you time to dress,' said Luke as he set Isobel down in the bedroom. He frowned suddenly, his eyes dark as they lingered on her bruises as she discarded the towel. 'I was too dazzled by your swimsuit to see those by the pool—and too desperate to make love to you last night,' he said, and dropped to his knees to set his lips to the marks. 'The man did that?' he demanded harshly.

'No. Wriggling out through the hut window did most of the damage.' Isobel brushed a hand over his wet curls. 'I must have a shower.'

He stood up to pull her close. 'I wish we were alone in the house,' he whispered.

She felt guilty for secretly agreeing. 'But we're not, and I'd love some coffee.'

Isobel rushed through her shower, then towelled her hair,

scrunched her fingers through it and left it to do its own thing while she got dressed again. Glowing after her swim, she collected her walking stick, determined to make it downstairs under her own steam. She was halfway there when Luke came out of his study to catch her in the act.

'You see?' she said defiantly and, with her hand on the intricate lacework of the carved banister, limped carefully down the last few stairs.

'You are a very determined woman,' he said, laughing, and, before she could prevent him, picked her up again. 'But I am a very determined man. You must take care until your ankle is bandaged again,' he informed her as he took her back to the reclining chairs. He sat down beside her and took her hand. 'So how do you really feel, *hriso mou*?'

Isobel gave him a straight look. 'Do you mean after my swim, or after making love with you last night?'

He frowned. 'I meant the last part. Because in my desire to celebrate life I think I was too demanding, *ne*? Did I hurt you?'

'No.' She flushed a little. 'I felt the same urge to celebrate, Luke.' She eyed him uneasily. 'Do you regret what happened between us?'

He raised the hand and pressed a kiss into her palm. 'How could I regret something so sublime, *kardia mou*?'

'But you were gone this morning.'

'For a very good reason. I woke up wanting to make love to you again, but exerted much self-control and let you sleep. Also, I thought you might not like Eleni to find me in your bed.'

'Very true,' she said with feeling, and shot a troubled look at him. 'Luke, will she think less of me for sleeping with you?'

'No,' he said emphatically. 'I told her—also Spiro—that I shall keep you with me night and day until you leave, to keep you safe. They agreed with great fervour. Spiro cannot forget the horror they felt the night you were stolen.' Luke smiled. 'They believe that fate sent such a lovely young lady to me.'

'Oh, dear,' said Isobel, mopping her eyes with a napkin. 'That's made me cry again. You won't believe this, but normally I hardly ever cry.'

'There is no sin in showing emotion, Isobel.' His eyes kindled. 'As you did in my arms last night. So dry your eyes, *agapi mou*. We must go down to Dr Riga now and ask him to strap your ankle.'

Isobel pulled a face. 'Is my hair a mess? I didn't do much to it after I washed it.'

'Those wild curls are very sexy. Leave them like that.' He handed her the stick. 'Be careful. I have worked hard—and braved much danger—to keep you safe.'

'I did some of the heavy lifting myself by getting out of that hut on the island,' she reminded him, laughing, then sobered suddenly. 'All the time I was praying for a miracle, and it happened. You came, Luke.'

'I did some praying myself on that boat trip,' he said grimly, and snatched her back into his arms to give her a hard, fleeting kiss. 'When I saw your hair as we came in to land I knew my prayers were answered.'

The trip to the clinic was made without incident and, after greetings with Dr Riga and the thorough check-up he insisted on, Isobel's ankle was strapped up and she was able to walk normally as she left, feeling secure in yellow espadrilles.

'I shall miss carrying you everywhere,' he said as he lifted her into the Cherokee.

So would she, Isobel admitted secretly. 'And I appreciated it,' she assured him, 'but it's good to feel independent again.'

'How you value your independence! But do not imagine you can go climbing down to any beaches,' he warned.

She pulled a face. 'No hardship there. I've rather lost my enthusiasm for beaches just now.'

'Good. Keep to peaceful strolls in the garden. When we get back I must ring Andres, and you can drink the tea Eleni is certain to have waiting for you. Ah,' he said, stopping the car. 'Alyssa is waving us down.'

Alyssa ran to lean in at the open window. *'Kalispera.'* She grinned at Luke. 'Just can't keep out of trouble, can you!'

'I do not seek it,' he assured her.

'You never try to avoid it either.' Alyssa smiled in apology at Isobel. 'Sorry I couldn't come up last night. Did you know what was going on?'

'Yes, I did.' Isobel exchanged a look with Luke. 'It was a huge relief to hear it was all over.'

'Come down to the taverna for a meal tonight and celebrate. My parents would love to see you both. Give Eleni the night off, Luke,' she coaxed.

He glanced at Isobel. 'Would you like that?'

With Alyssa waiting, there was only one answer Isobel felt she could make. 'I would, yes.'

'Are you sure about this?' said Luke as they drove off. 'I was hoping to have you all to myself this evening.'

'We needn't stay long,' she consoled him, and smiled up at him as she stroked a finger along his muscular thigh. 'We can go to bed early when we get home.'

As soon as the car stopped, both Eleni and Spiro hurried to hear the doctor's verdict.

'I hope you weren't cooking anything special tonight, Eleni,' said Isobel anxiously. 'Alyssa is keen for us to dine at the taverna.'

Eleni shook her head, smiling, and led Isobel indoors to sit on a chair at the veranda table. 'I not even shop yet. Spiro take me now.'

Isobel poured herself a cup of tea as Eleni hurried off, but she'd managed only a sip before Luke bent over her. 'How fast can you drink that?'

'Why?'

He smiled persuasively as the car started up outside. 'We shall be alone in the house for hours, and you look tired. You need a rest. So do I.'

'In that case, pour my tea on a flower bed or wherever. I'm hot, anyway.'

'So am I, *hriso mou*,' he said huskily, and picked her up.

'I can walk now,' she protested, but he shook his head and hurried up the stairs with her.

'Too slow. Why waste time?'

There was so little of it before she left, Isobel was in full agreement as Luke carried her into her cool, airy bedroom and immediately began undressing her.

'You're in a big hurry,' she protested breathlessly as he flung their garments in all directions.

'Only over this part,' he said, and knelt naked on the bed to lean over her, his eyes gleaming down into hers. 'I promise to love you as slowly as possible.'

The words spoken in that husky, irresistible voice, coupled with the knowledge that they were alone in the big house in the hot languor of the afternoon, created an aphrodisiac effect new to Isobel. As with so many other things since her arrival on Chyros.

'It's so quiet, we could be alone in the world,' she whispered, quivering at the touch of skilled, inciting hands.

'Just the two of us, *hriso mou*, like Adam and Eve. But with no serpents in our paradise any more.' He caressed her breasts, kissing her softly and nibbling gently on her lower lip, then as her lips parted his kisses became fierce and his hands more urgent and she threaded her fingers through his hair, holding him closer, responding with heat and fire which brought him to full, triumphant arousal. At last, when they were both trembling with the desperation to mate, he reared up over her, his face stern with the desire he was trying to hold in check.

'I can't keep my promise,' he panted, and she gave him a smile the original Adam would have recognised.

'Break it, then,' she whispered, and gave a gasp of pure, unadulterated pleasure as he obeyed.

This time there was no gradual acceleration of their loving. Isobel was as wild as Luke from the start, and all too soon found herself throbbing in the throes of a climax which overtook her several seconds before his body collapsed on hers in his own convulsive release. She lay stunned as her heart began to slow down, but at last, when oxygen became a necessity, she pushed at Luke's shoulders and in one movement he lifted himself from her and rolled so that she lay on top of him instead.

'Better?' he asked, smiling at her, lazy-eyed, as he held her in place, skin to skin.

'I liked having you lie on me, but in the end I couldn't breathe.' She bent her head to kiss him. 'Will you be able to hear when the car comes back?'

'Spiro will gun the engine down to the house, making as much noise as possible,' he assured her, grinning.

'You told him to do that?'

'No. Spiro is a man, and Greek. I had no need to tell him.' Isobel sniffed. 'I suppose he's used to it.'

His eyebrow arched. 'And what, *kyria* Isobel, do you mean by that?'

She felt suddenly very vulnerable, sprawled naked, and by the sudden tightening of his arms, with no hope of getting free. Her eyes fell, unable to meet the look of hot possession in his.

'I have never brought a woman to the Villa Medusa before,' he said with emphasis. 'This is my private retreat. Or it was—'

'Until I trespassed,' she finished for him. 'Let me up, please.'

'No,' he said flatly. 'Not until you atone for doubting me.'

She eyed him stormily and tried to wriggle free, but he held her fast and too late she realised that her attempts to escape had such an inflammatory effect on him she was suddenly flat on her back again and Luke was holding her prisoner in an entirely different way.

'All—right, I—believe you,' she said with difficulty.

'Too late. You must pay the penalty,' he said roughly.

And, sooner than she would have believed possible, Luke was making love to her again, with an added edge that sent delicious thrills through her body as he claimed it with mastery which sent them both rocketing to another climax even more powerful than the first.

'So do you believe me now?' he panted as he pulled away, holding her so close against him Isobel could feel his heartbeat as his taut body began to relax.

'Yes. I do. But you have other women in Athens—'

'In the past, yes. But there is no one in my life now, I swear. I was brought up to tell the truth, Isobel.' He turned her face up to his. 'And so were you, *ne*? So tell me, *agapi mou*, are your feelings warmer to me now?'

'Warmer than what, exactly?'

'You were very hostile towards me at first.'

She sniffed. 'Only because you were so hostile to me, Lukas Andreadis.'

He smoothed the uneven lock of hair back from her forehead. 'When you return, will you tell your friend Joanna about me?'

'Of course. She'll be only too glad that I met someone who could make me forget the Gavin episode. Joanna never liked him. Neither did March, her husband.'

'You like your friend's husband?'

'Very much. Seeing them so happy together almost changes my mind about marriage.'

His eyes narrowed intently. 'But not enough to want it for yourself.'

'Never. As I told you before, marriage doesn't appeal to me in the slightest. I enjoy my independence too much—' She tensed as she heard the Jeep approaching the house. 'Luke, hurry, they're back!'

CHAPTER ELEVEN

THEY were late leaving for the taverna. Isobel had taken a shower as soon as Luke left her, and then collapsed on her bed to sleep for a while, while Luke spent the time in consultation with Andres before standing lost in thought under his own shower.

So Isobel disliked the idea of marriage. Which was good, because so did he. But there was nothing to keep them from being lovers. He smiled as he lay on his bed, which was a lot larger than the one in the guest room. He made a note to bring Isobel here to sleep with him once he had persuaded her to stay for a while. The heat and pleasure of lovemaking was something he'd experienced often enough in his life, but in the past it had soon died away, leaving nothing to replace it other than fond regret when the parting of the ways arrived, as it always did. But Isobel was different. Making love with her surpassed all other experiences in his life to such an extent it seemed to touch his soul. But he also took great pleasure in her company as they talked and ate and swam and simply spent time together. He would make her see that leaving him was not an option yet. But his persuasion must be subtle. He must accustom her to the idea by degrees, paint an irresistible picture of what they could have together. But it was best to wait until the agonising moment of their parting when her only answer could be yes. Miss Isobel James must be convinced beyond all doubt that fate had not only sent her to him, but meant her to stay here with him for the foreseeable future.

The evening at the taverna was lively. Luke and Isobel were welcomed with open arms, with much admiration for Luke's part in the dramatic rescue of the beautiful Miss James. Nikos Nicolaides, in particular, felt a proprietorial pleasure about this, since Lukas had met the lady because she came to spend a holiday in one of his properties.

The evening was a further celebration of life for Isobel, a time to rejoice with people who so obviously thought the world not only of Luke, but had felt the same about his mother.

'They're all very fond of you,' Isobel told him on the way home.

'And I of them. This is why Chyros is such a special place to me. People here remember how hard I had to work to achieve my success; therefore no one resents it.' His voice dropped a tone. 'And you, Isobel? Has your experience here turned you against my island?'

'No, of course not. I'll always treasure my memories of Eleni and Spiro, and Alyssa and her family. And you.' She drew in a deep breath. 'I'd planned to do so many things while I was here, take a trip to Serifos and some of the other islands, also paint a few watercolours I could put on sale back home in the gallery.'

'But the only trip you made was against your will, to a barren island with no legends of any kind. So I shall take you wherever you want to go,' he promised as they turned down the tree-lined drive to the villa. 'I spoke to Andres earlier, by the way. The Karras sisters finally confessed in their more lucid moments that they hired both men, who are workers on the Karras family estate up north.'

'Did the women order the kidnapper to kill me once they got the ransom?' asked Isobel as he lifted her out of the jeep.

Luke held her tightly for a moment, kissed her fiercely, then set her on her feet. 'If they did, they chose the wrong man to commit murder for them. Which is why he told me where to find you. Not that it mattered, because I had found you first.'

'Thank God,' said Isobel, and buried her face against his chest. 'I confess that I was bit frightened, Luke.'

'Enough to give you nightmares,' he agreed as they went into the house. 'I think I should guard you from them again tonight, *ne*?'

'Yes, *please*,' she said fervently as Luke bent to pick her up. 'I can walk now.'

He slid an arm round her waist. 'Like this, then.'

Isobel leaned against him happily. 'Like this,' she agreed with a sigh. 'I had such a good time tonight, Luke.'

'So did I, *hriso mou*. Are you tired?'

'Just pleasantly so.'

'Where would you like to go tomorrow?'

'I'd like to explore Chyros properly,' she said eagerly. 'Since I've been here at the villa I've seen only quick glimpses of it. And the day you rescued me I travelled back to the villa rolled up in a rug like Cleopatra.'

Luke closed her bedroom door behind them and took her in his arms. 'You shall do whatever you want tomorrow, Isobel, I promise. But tonight we do what I want. Tell me you want it, too, *kardia mou*.'

'You know I do,' she said honestly, her eyes falling before the blaze in his as he picked her up to put her on the bed.

Later, when Isobel was quiet at last in Luke's arms, he lay with his face buried in her hair for a long time before he raised his head to look into her heavy eyes.

'It was never like this for me with others,' he said in a tone which melted her bones.

She heaved in a long unsteady breath, wanting passionately to believe him. 'Nor for me, either.' She raised an eyebrow. 'Though there have been fewer *others* by far in *my* life, Lukas Andreadis.'

'I can tell,' he said with satisfaction.

'How?'

'Because you are so plainly—and enchantingly—surprised by the joy we find together, *ne*?'

Surprised seemed hardly the word. Luke's caresses had been revelations, not only in themselves, but in her wildly un-inhibited response to them. 'I said it was different with you,' she reminded him.

'Because I am a good lover?'

'You want marks for your performance?' she demanded, laughing, and he smiled smugly.

'No. Your response was accolade enough, *agapi mou*.'

Isobel laughed again, and Luke rolled over, hugging her to him.

'Now we sleep. Tomorrow we explore my island.'

And soon after that she would be leaving. Secure in Luke's arms, Isobel firmly shut all thought of the future away and concentrated on the blissful present.

The programme Luke had mapped out was everything that Isobel could have wished for except that it made the time go by far too quickly. He took her on a tour of Chyros the next day, as promised, and drove up beyond the villa, following a road which wound up through olive groves and stands of pines. They passed a monastery, with a white dome glimmer-ing like a pearl in its crown of cypress, and soon afterwards Luke halted on a promontory of rock near the highest point of the island, with a view of such beauty spread out below Isobel wished she had brushes and paint to capture it.

'You can make a painting from here next time you come,' said Luke, reading her mind.

Her face fell. 'I won't be coming back.'

He shook his head, the sun catching glints of gold in the bronze curls. 'You will return for Alyssa's wedding, *ne*?'

'No, Luke. I can't expect my boss to let me take more time off. And I need the job.'

He gave her a long introspective look, then started the car without further argument. Which left Isobel more forlorn than ever. A touch more coaxing would have been nice.

Over dinner Luke gave Isobel details of the conversation he'd had with Andres while she was reading on the veranda earlier. 'I am sorry it took the entire afternoon, but there was much to catch up on with the airline, also with my freighters. And,' he added dramatically, 'Andres had more news of the Karras sisters. Loss of the ransom money, added to claustro-phobia at being locked up separately, tipped them over the edge into insanity. They have been committed to a secure mental in-stitution.' He leaned to grasp Isobel's hand. 'So you can sleep easy now, *agapi mou*.' His eyes narrowed suddenly as he gazed out over the pool. 'Do you want a trip in the *Athena* tomorrow?'

'Why? Is there something you'd rather do?'

'Zeus, yes,' he said with feeling, and smiled into her eyes. 'I think Eleni and Spiro should take the day off tomorrow to visit family.'

Isobel frowned. 'I thought they didn't have a family.'

'No children, but they have numerous relatives all over the island. They must be anxious to bring them up to date on what happened here at the villa. Eleni can leave food for us and Spiro can take the Cherokee.'

She felt her colour rise. 'Won't they want to know why?'

Luke got up and drew her to her feet. 'They will think I want you to myself for the last day before you leave. Which is the simple truth. Do you want that, Isobel?'

'Of course I do.'

'Not,' he said very deliberately, 'that I mean to spend the whole day in bed, you understand. It will be enough just to be alone with you by the pool, and walk in the garden, and simply spend every minute possible together. Though I hope—need—to spend *some* of those minutes making love with you. But,' he added nobly, 'we can still go out in the boat if you prefer.'

Isobel stood on tiptoe and put her arms round his neck. 'I prefer your plan,' she assured him.

And a whole day spent this way, thought Luke as he rubbed his cheek against her hair, was all it would take to convince Isobel that she must stay, to ensure many more such days together.

Isobel's last full day on Chyros with Luke would have been perfect, bar one inescapable element—that she would be leaving the next morning. As he wanted, they spent almost every minute of the day together. As the sound of the Cherokee's engine dwindled into the distance, taking Spiro and Eleni away, Luke smiled at Isobel with deep satisfaction.

'Alone at last!'

'So now we talk,' she said firmly. 'Tell me all about your life, Luke.'

'Not all of it is exciting, Isobel,' he warned, and began with the freighter which had been his starting point, out of which he'd built up a fleet so commercially successful it enabled him to take over the airline Melina Andreadis had considered her own personal property. Now it was his, he informed Isobel, it would soon have a very different reputation for luxury and dependability instead of the cheap, too frequent flights of her day. 'I have an apartment in Athens, also one in Thessaloniki. You would like it there. Visitors rate it as a very hip, cool city. And from there you can explore the mountains, go to the oracle at Delphi and to Mount Olympus, the home of the gods.'

'I'd love to do that one day,' said Isobel wistfully, getting to her feet.

'You want to go back to bed?' he said, kissing her.

'No way, *kyrie*,' she retorted, laughing, and stripped off her sundress. 'Let's swim.'

They swam and sunbathed, ate the salad lunch Eleni had left for them, then Luke got up, holding out his hand. 'Now we go to bed.'

A long time later, when they were holding each other close in the sweet, languorous aftermath of passion, tears trickled down Isobel's cheeks.

'Why are you crying?' demanded Luke, kissing them away.

'Because I'm happy,' lied Isobel, and concealed a sharp pang of pain with a yawn.

'Sleep, *hriso mou*,' he said in a tone like a caress.

It seemed a wanton waste of the time left to them, but Isobel was so tired she obeyed, and woke later to find him tickling her nose with a lock of her own hair.

'I will leave you to your shower, then we take a walk in the garden while the sun goes down. And after that we drink a glass of wine while we watch the stars come out to play.' He kissed her swiftly. 'Ten minutes, *ne*?'

Isobel was pleased in one way that Luke hadn't wanted to share her shower. It was not the most graceful of procedures for someone balanced on one foot. Though it would have been something to look back on, she thought wistfully. Also a first for her. With Luke she wanted to experience everything possible between a man and woman in love… Her breath caught. Love, the four letter word. It was pointless to pretend she wasn't madly in love with Luke. But did he feel the same? Their time together had been packed so full of incident there had been an inevitable greenhouse effect on their relationship. Luke left her in no doubt that he wanted her physically. But whether love was part of his equation was hard to tell. Not that it mattered. Tomorrow she was going home and would never see him again.

Luke was waiting outside on the landing when Isobel emerged in a brief, filmy slip dress the colour of her eyes. He gave her a look which brought a blush to her face, and took her hand as they went downstairs together.

'Why didn't you just come in to wait for me, Luke?'

'Because I would have wanted to lay you down on that bed again,' he informed her huskily. 'And you would have objected because you look so perfect in that delightful dress.'

Isobel smiled at him as they reached the veranda. 'I'm glad you like it. I've been saving it for a special occasion.'

'Every night with you is a special occasion,' he said, and took her hand to stroll out into the garden. 'How is the foot, Isobel?'

'It's fine now, really. Which is good, because it has to get me home tomorrow.'

'Let me fly you to the airport in the helicopter,' he urged, but she shook her head.

'No, thanks. I'll go back on the boat, the way I came. The journey will get me back to normal by degrees.' She smiled wryly. 'Life at home is going to seem very humdrum from now on.'

'Who will meet you at the airport?'

'Joanna. I'll send her a text just before I board the plane.' Isobel breathed in the scent of the flowers as they skirted the pool to make for the row of Aleppo pines lining the cliff edge. She gazed down on the sunset-gilded beach. 'It's such a short time since you found me down there, yet in other ways it seems as though I've known you forever.'

'I believe we met in another life,' said Luke, and put his arm round her. 'Come. We shall go back and toast the setting sun with a glass of wine.'

Later, Isobel had little appetite for the *mezedes* Eleni had left them; though the appetizers were as delicious as all her food. 'I'm not so hungry tonight,' she said apologetically.

'Nor I.' He raised her hand to his and kissed it. 'Isobel, I need to talk to you. And the best place for that is bed.'

'Pillow talk?'

He shook his head. 'Vital, important talk.'

Isobel disliked the sound of this; her misgivings intensified when Luke opened the bedroom door for her, but remained outside. 'I will join you in a few moments,' he said, surprising her. 'Tonight, it is better you undress yourself.'

His tone left Isobel so uneasy that, after undressing quickly, she put a nightgown over her head. Nudity was inappropriate for a serious talk. She went back to sit on the bed, and while she waited for Luke sent a text to Joanna to confirm that she was returning tomorrow on schedule, and would ring just before boarding the plane.

Luke arrived as she closed her phone. 'Who were you telephoning?' He was wearing a towelling robe for once, and added to Isobel's misgivings by taking the chair beside the bed instead of joining her on it.

'Just a text to Joanna, to confirm the travel arrangements.' Isobel eyed him narrowly. 'Is something wrong, Luke?'

He scowled. 'You are leaving tomorrow and you ask me if something is wrong?' When she said nothing, he leaned forward, his face urgent. 'It is necessary that I talk to you like this, without touching, so you know that my words are not said in the heat of the moment.'

She stiffened. 'Could you just get on and say these words, Luke. You're worrying me.'

His eyes softened. 'That was not my intention. In fact,' he added heavily, 'I think I have made a mistake. It would have been better to talk after making love.'

'For heaven's sake, Luke,' she said in desperation. 'Tell me what's wrong!'

'Nothing wrong, *agapi mou*. If we had more time together I would have waited longer to lead up to this, but you are leaving tomorrow. What I have to say is very simple. I want so much more of you than your holiday has allowed me,' he said with emphasis, his eyes urgent on hers. 'Listen to my plan, Isobel. I shall buy you a house in Athens, or Thessaloniki, whichever you prefer. You can paint there as much as you like. I will give you anything your heart desires, and spend as much time with you as I can.' He leaned nearer. 'Think of all the happy days—and nights—we could enjoy together, Isobel.'

She thought of them in silence so prolonged he grew restive. 'Are you serious?' she said at last.

Luke's eyebrows shot together. 'The idea does not please you?'

Isobel took in a deep breath. 'Luke, we come from different cultures, so I don't know quite where I stand on this. Are you asking me to be one of your pillow friends?'

'No! There will be no one else in my life when you come to me, Isobel.'

'So my official job description would be mistress?'

He smiled indulgently. 'Not my mistress, Isobel—my lover!'

Same thing. 'And what would happen when you marry?'

'There is no fear of that. Like you, I do not want marriage. But I want *you* so much it is agony to part with you, *hriso mou.*' His eyes locked with hers. 'Say yes, Isobel. Say you will come to me.'

She sighed and shook her head. 'I'm sorry. The answer's no.'

Luke leapt to his feet, his eyes incredulous, as though he couldn't believe she'd refused. Then they hardened as his face set into the familiar blank mask. 'I have made a most humiliating mistake. I believed you had come to care for me, and shared my pain at the thought of parting. Neither of us desires marriage; therefore my plan seemed the perfect solution. I was obviously wrong.' His mirthless smile sent shivers down her spine. 'In time I shall be able to laugh at myself for such hubris. But not yet. Goodnight, Isobel.'

She stared in anguish as the door closed behind him, then burrowed into the pillows feeling as though her world was breaking in pieces around her. At last she went into the bathroom to wash her tear-stained face. She had expected to spend their last night in bed together but, as that wasn't going to happen, she might as well pack. She took her bags from the wardrobe and began folding clothes and rolling up underwear, putting shoes in what polythene bags she had left, and reminded herself that her drawing materials were downstairs and would have to be packed in the morning.

She worked like an automaton, her brain still reeling from the shock of Luke's proposition. She might be madly in love with him, but Luke's offer—or demand, more like it—would mean uprooting herself from her life, and parting from her friends and everything familiar. And for what? Marriage was a tricky enough relationship, but the insecurity of living as Luke's mistress, lover, or whatever, was out of the question. He obviously intended her to lack for nothing, which probably meant an allowance of some kind. And, with money involved, the whole idea left a nasty taste in her mouth. Besides, what would happen when the arrangement came to an end? She might love Luke with a depth and passion which almost frightened her, but she valued her independence—and her self-respect—too highly to agree to such a dubious arrangement. Even with Lukas Andreadis.

Not that there was any point in beating herself up about it because none of that was going to happen. Right now, she just had to go home, back to her old life, and learn to live without Lukas Andreadis as part of it. But to part from him this way, like enemies instead of lovers, was cutting her to the heart. If they were never going to see each other again she desperately wanted—needed—one last memory to look back on when she was home, alone and lonely.

Before she could change her mind, Isobel limped as fast as she could out onto the landing to knock on Luke's door. When there was no answer she turned away blindly but ran into a hard, familiar body and Luke snatched her up in his arms, kissing her tears away as he carried her back to her room.

'What did you want, Isobel?' he demanded as he laid her on the bed.

No point in lying. 'I couldn't bear to leave without making up.'

'Nor could I.' He shrugged off his robe, took her nightgown over her head and covered her body with his, devouring her with hot, desperate kisses she responded to with such impassioned fervour they surged together at once, their emotions running so high after their quarrel they achieved culmination so swiftly Isobel shook in Luke's arms with the force of it.

Luke looked down into her swollen eyes. 'Does this mean you have changed your mind?' he panted.

'No.' She sucked in a deep breath. 'Though you could be forgiven for thinking I had by the way I—I—'

'Participated so joyously in our loving?'

She gave a choked little laugh. 'Shamelessly, you mean.'

'There is no shame in a man and a woman giving each other such rapture, *agapi mou*,' he assured her and held her close, rubbing his cheek against hers. 'Think of the joy we can give each other in future, Isobel. You may run away tomorrow, but I shall not give up. We were created to be together. When you were stolen from me I was in hell thinking I had lost you.' He kissed her fiercely. 'Fate sent you to me, and what I find I keep. It is useless to fight fate, *hriso mou*. You are mine.'

CHAPTER TWELVE

As the first light of dawn appeared Luke propped himself on one elbow to look down into Isobel's face.

'I will give you six weeks,' he said imperiously. 'At the end of that time you will come back to me, or I will fetch you.'

'You're very sure of yourself, Lukas Andreadis.'

'It is the way I succeed in life.' His eyes glittered. 'I want you, Isobel. You are clear on this?'

She smiled wryly. 'Yes. But what happens if I say no again at the end of six weeks?'

'You will not,' he said simply, and drew her down into his arms. 'I will not allow it.'

It was a day of painful partings, starting with Eleni and Spiro, and even Milos, who came to say goodbye. Before boarding the boat there was a brief stop at the clinic for Isobel to say her goodbyes to Dr Riga, then more at the taverna, to Alyssa and her parents. By the time Luke carried her bags onto the boat, Isobel was desperate for him to leave her alone with her misery. But, to her surprise, Luke sat beside her, his arm very firmly around her waist.

'I shall come to the airport with you,' he said in a tone that told Isobel not to argue.

'But how will you get back?'

'I shall stay in Athens.' He tightened his arm as the boat moved out to sea. 'I will need much work to fill my days once I am without you, *kardia mou*.' He smiled crookedly. 'Did you really think I'd let you go to the airport alone? You need someone to carry your bags, *ne*?'

Isobel leaned against him, her heart already wanting her to change her mind and tell him she would come back and do, and be, anything he wanted. But in the end her head took over and kept her emotions firmly under wraps, even through the torment of parting with Luke at the airport.

The flight home gave Isobel much-needed time to think. Although Luke had given her six weeks to get used to the idea, she already knew that she could never agree to the role of part-time playmate. If he'd simply asked her to live with him, share his life in his Athens flat, or in Thessaloniki, or any-where else, she would have said yes without hesitation. But languishing alone in some house in either city, waiting for him to spare time for her, was out of the question, no matter how much she loved him. Which she did, passionately. The wrench of parting from Luke had been so painful she felt as though she'd left her heart behind with him.

Isobel's spirits rose at the airport as she saw Joanna waiting for her. Glowing and vital, chestnut hair gleaming, her friend was waving madly as Isobel steered a luggage trolley towards her. After a brief explanation of the walking stick, Isobel stayed put as ordered while Jo fetched the car.

'Now then, Isobel James,' said Jo, once they were on the motorway heading for home. 'The one time you cut loose on your own on holiday you come back injured. Give me every last detail, please.'

But Isobel shook her head. 'I'd rather you weren't driving when I do. Are you in a hurry to get back to Arnborough?'

'No.' Jo shot her a worried look. 'March knew we'd want to catch up. I'm yours for the evening.'

'Great. Let's buy some food on the way home and talk over supper.'

The gallery was closed for the day by the time they arrived. Isobel unlocked her private side door, gritting her teeth as she confronted two flights of steep stairs. She hooked the walking stick through the straps of her backpack and picked up her tote, but Jo insisted on making two trips to carry the shopping and the rest of the luggage up to the flat. She even took over the unpacking while Isobel first sent a text message to Luke to announce her arrival, and then sat down at the kitchen table to make sandwiches. When they were ready Jo planted herself in the chair opposite and fixed Isobel with a steely eye.

'Right. Talk,' she ordered.

Isobel told her tale as dispassionately as possible. Other than the occasional exclamation, Joanna heard her out in silence, then sat staring at her friend, stupefied.

'What a *story*,' she said faintly and reached out a hand to touch the ragged lock of hair beside her friend's ear. 'Thank God I didn't know what was happening.' She looked Isobel in the eye. 'And this man—'

'Lukas Andreadis.'

'Yes, him. He wants you to be his *mistress*?'

'Don't sound so shocked!'

'Well, it's a hell of a cheek,' said Jo impatiently. 'I thought only married men had mistresses. So what was your reaction?'

Isobel smiled ruefully. 'When he first brought it up I turned him down flat, and he stormed off in a temper. Luke is used to women throwing themselves at him, so to have one say no to him was quite a shock.'

'That type, is he! So is your answer still no now you've had time to get used to the idea?'

'He's given me six weeks. After which I am to overcome my qualms about leaving everything familiar and dear to me, and let him install me in some love-nest in Athens or Thessaloniki, my choice. There I am to paint my pictures and wait around until he has time to visit me.'

Joanna's jaw dropped. 'Which century is he living in? So what happens if you say no again?'

Isobel heaved a sigh. 'He has this Greek thing about fate. Because he found me stranded on his beach he believes fate handed me to him on a platter, so to speak. He's so certain of this he swears he'll never give up on me.'

'Wild!' said Jo, impressed. 'So, if women throw themselves at him, I take it the man's no turn-off in the looks department?'

Isobel smiled as she took the portrait of Luke from her luggage. 'There he is. Like no other man I've ever met. And I'm so much in love with him it's going to be hell to say no when he wants his answer.'

The weeks that followed Isobel's return home were taxing in multiple ways, over and above the almost physical pain of missing Luke. Working in the busy gallery was tiring enough normally, even with the help of the art student who came in part-time, but with a weak ankle still in the mix she was exhausted by the end of her working day. And before her holiday she had thought nothing of living in a flat over a gallery full of valuable paintings. But now, even though the high-end security system was allegedly burglar-proof, she was nervous at night and found it hard to sleep. Even when she did she sometimes woke in fright from a new nightmare, fighting to remove an imaginary cloth from her face. With no Luke in the flesh to keep her safe in the night, his phone calls were the high points of her life. And, as he never ceased to remind her, the six weeks he had given her would soon be up.

Luke passed on messages from Alyssa, who ordered him to give Isobel all the news of the island and to do his utmost to persuade her to come back there for her wedding. Strange, thought Isobel, how she could be homesick for a place where she'd spent such a short time. She gave Luke messages to pass back to Alyssa and felt a pang when she heard that he was returning to Chyros for Eleni's birthday, which he said with significance, would also mark the end of the six weeks.

Isobel posted off a cashmere shawl to Eleni as a birthday gift. Then, after spending hours over composing a painful letter to Luke, she sent it off, got rid of her mobile phone and bought a new one.

'Why on earth have you done that?' demanded Joanna.

'My time's up, but I just couldn't face telling Luke my answer's no, so I wrote to him instead. I left the address off the letter and then ditched the phone so he can't contact me,' she said wearily.

'You've made up your mind, then?'

'Yes. It was never on, really.' Isobel gave a mirthless little chuckle. 'Deep down, it seems, I'm the product of my grandparents' upbringing.'

Having made her decision, Isobel hid Luke's portrait away, but she hung the watercolour of his beach in the gallery with a 'sold' sticker on it. The painting aroused such interest it resulted in new commissions Isobel welcomed with open arms, both from an extra income point of view and as a means to fill time, which hung heavy since her return from holiday.

Jo came into town once a week to take her out to a meal, a ritual she'd kept up since her marriage. One evening her husband March came with her, and on another occasion Isobel managed to catch Josh and Leo Carey with rare matching time off from the hospital, which resulted in a hilarious evening, as always when the four of them were together. Jo also passed on an invitation from her parents to spend an entire day at their home one Sunday. 'March is coming, too, and you can play with the children as much as you like,' she said firmly.

Isobel accepted only too happily, glad of the chance to see young Kitty and Tom, Jo's irresistible little siblings. The working week she could manage. But when the gallery was shut on Sundays she had too much time for the burning question of whether she had made the biggest mistake of her life in cutting herself off from Luke.

Two months after her return from Greece, Isobel was about to lock up for the day when a car drew up right outside the gallery. She went out to say that it was a no parking zone, then froze, the colour draining from her face as the driver got out and stood looking at her over the top of the car.

Oh, God. Isobel's mouth dried and her heart began to pound as the familiar black eyes locked with hers. Her gut reaction was to run inside and lock the door. Instead, she stood her ground and smiled brightly. 'Why, hello. This is a surprise.'

'And not a pleasant one, I think,' said Luke, locking the car. He wore beautiful suede boots, heavy sweater and jeans, all very different from his usual garb on Chyros. But his face was the handsome mask she remembered only too well. Whatever Luke was thinking, he was giving nothing away as he crossed the kerb to join her. 'But surely you expected this after the letter you wrote, Isobel?'

'No, I didn't,' she said truthfully. How on earth had he found her?

'Have you finished for the day?'

'Yes. I was just about to lock up. Would you like to come in?'

Luke followed her inside, watching as she closed the door. Conscious of the black eyes following her every move, Isobel punched in the numbers on the security pad beside it and shot bolts home at the top of the door and again at the base.

'Perhaps you'd care to look round the paintings while I make coffee,' she said brightly. 'Or would you prefer a drink? I have some wine—'

He shook his head. 'I would like to look at the paintings. Is any of your work here, Isobel?'

'Yes. I have a little section all to myself.' When she made no move to direct him, Luke strolled away on a tour of the artwork she prided herself she displayed to the best advantage with subtle lighting against the contrast of the gallery's dark red walls.

Luke paused when he reached the far end of the room and looked in silence at a collection of Isobel's watercolours. 'You have sold your painting of my beach.'

'No. I put a sold sticker on it to show it wasn't for sale.'

'You intend to keep it?'

'Yes.'

'Why?'

She looked at him steadily. 'As a souvenir of my holiday. I once told you—though you didn't believe me at the time— that where others take holiday snaps, I sketch or paint.'

Luke's mask slipped a fraction as he walked back to her. 'Spiro showed me the drawing you made of my face. It flatters me.'

She shrugged. 'I thought it was pretty accurate, myself.

Though I rarely do portraits. Not my field.' Lord, this was painful. Why didn't he yell at her, or at least tell her why he'd come?

'Your hair is shorter,' he remarked. 'I prefer it long.'

Her eyes flashed. 'So do I. Losing a chunk of it was hardly my fault.'

'No, it was mine,' he agreed grimly and moved closer, his eyes softening. 'You look tired, Isobel.'

'I've been busy today.'

'You have no help here?'

'I have an assistant, but he left a short while ago.' Tired of small talk, Isobel cut to the chase. 'I didn't put an address on my letter, so how did you find me?'

Luke's smile set her teeth on edge. 'For a while I was so furious I had no wish to find you. But, after seeing your painting of my pool, my faithful Andres, who found working with me very difficult after I received your letter, suggested that you might sell your work through a website. The rest was easy. Had you forgotten the power of the Internet, Isobel?'

'No. I just took it for granted that once you received my letter you'd be so angry you'd just put me out of your life and forget me.'

'It was my first reaction,' he admitted. 'Out of all the emotions that besieged me, the most violent was anger because you were a coward, Isobel. You rejected me by letter. But my fury soon gave way to a desire to hear you say no to me, face to face. And to give me your real explanation.' He moved closer. 'So here I am.'

Isobel looked at him in silence for a moment, then crossed to the control panel. 'I leave the security lights on for the paintings in the windows, but at this hour I switch off the rest.' She turned with a polite smile. 'Perhaps you'd like to come up to my flat. I'm desperate for a cup of tea.' Inane, but the truth. Her mouth was so dry it was hard to swallow.

'*Efcharisto*, Isobel. Then later I will take you out to dine.'

She made no response to that and opened the private door leading to her stairs. 'Two flights up, I'm afraid.'

'Is your ankle better? These stairs must have been difficult for a while when you first returned,' he commented, following her up.

A lot of things had been difficult. Most of them still were. 'My ankle's fine now,' she said politely. When she reached the small landing at the head of the stairs she opened the door of her sitting room and waved him inside. 'Do sit down while I make tea.'

Left alone to inspect them, Luke eyed his surroundings with interest. The artist in Isobel had a flair for the dramatic. A peacock-blue throw draped a jade velvet couch, and ruby and gold silk cushions glowed on a leather armchair. At strategic points around the room small tables of varying design held piles of books and lamps with vivid shades.

A jewel box of a room, thought Luke, then turned as the jewel who lived in it backed into the room with a tray. 'Let me,' he said, and took the tray from her. 'Where shall I put it?'

Isobel cleared a space on a table alongside the sofa and Luke set the tray down with care, feeling very male and clumsy in the feminine room. 'Try the chair,' she invited. 'I made coffee for you, by the way.'

'*Efcharisto.*' He took the cup from her and put it safe on a table alongside the couch, afraid that if he moved too suddenly he would knock something over. 'So. Why would you not come to me, Isobel?' he said baldly.

She sipped some tea before she answered. 'I did consider it—I thought about it long and hard. Then something happened which made it impossible. So I wrote the letter.'

Luke snatched up his coffee cup, ignoring the sting as the liquid scalded his mouth. 'You met another man?'

'No.' Isobel took in a deep breath, wishing her heart would stop banging around in her chest. 'I found out I'm pregnant—I'm having a baby, Luke.'

He looked as though she'd punched him in the stomach. 'Is it mine?' He sat very still, every muscle in his body tense as he watched the colour leach from her face.

'No,' she said after a taut pause.

'Whose, then?' he demanded, his pallor outdoing hers.

'Mine.'

His jaw clenched. 'You told me you took care of birth control yourself.'

Isobel stabbed him with a glacial blue glare. 'I did. But I was kidnapped, remember. The man didn't give me time to pack my pills.' Suddenly she sprang up to run to the bathroom and stayed there until she was sure her stomach meant to behave. She would have given much to remain locked in the bathroom for the foreseeable future, but eventually she went out in answer to Luke's urgent knock on the door.

He barred her way as she made to brush past him. 'You are sure of this?'

'Yes. But don't worry; I'm not asking *you* for anything.' Her eyes blazed like sapphires into his. 'Your knee-jerk reaction to my glad news only confirms how right I was to finish things between us.'

Luke seized her by the wrists. 'I apologise, Isobel. I said such a bad thing because the thought of you with another man's child was a stab to my heart.'

'How melodramatic,' she said dully, and detached her hands. 'Perhaps you'd be good enough to leave now, and go back to wherever you're staying. I'm very tired.'

'But we have much to discuss,' he said hotly. 'How do you expect me to sleep after such news?'

She shrugged indifferently. 'Frankly, Lukas Andreadis, I don't care a toss whether you sleep or not. Just *go*.'

'Of course,' he said stiffly. 'I will burden you with my presence no longer. But,' he added in a tone which made her toes curl, 'when I return, Isobel, we shall talk.'

After the menace in Luke's parting shot Isobel decided to postpone supper for a while. 'I'll eat something later,' she promised, patting her stomach. 'Sorry about your dad. I'm afraid it's just you and me, babe.' But even if she managed some supper she had little hope of getting any sleep later with the prospect of Luke's return visit hanging over her. Hopefully, he would come at a reasonable enough hour the next day to allow recovery from her daily date with morning sickness.

The bell on Isobel's door rang later while she was drying her hair after her bath. She frowned. She wasn't expecting Jo, or one of the Careys. And her boss, the owner of the gallery, was sunning himself in Mauritius. When the bell rang again she picked up the receiver on her intercom.

'Let me in, Isobel,' said Luke's unmistakable tones.

'I didn't expect you back tonight,' she said coldly.

'Nevertheless, I am here. And attracting attention. Open the door,' he ordered.

Isobel pressed the release button, cursing because she had no time to dress. She ran into the bedroom for her old blue velour robe, tied the sash tightly, raked her fingers through her damp curls, then took a deep breath and opened her sitting room door to Luke's knock.

He was wearing different clothes, he was newly shaved and his hair, like hers, was damp.

'Have you eaten?' he demanded, eyeing the robe.

'No. We weren't hungry.'

A pulse throbbed at the corner of his mouth at the 'we'. 'You must eat,' he said disapprovingly. 'I will take you to my hotel for dinner.'

She shook her head. 'I'd rather not be seen with you in public.'

Colour flared along his cheekbones. 'Why? Am I not dressed suitably?'

'This is a small town. People know me here. Questions would be asked.'

'That you would not care to answer,' he flung at her.

'Why are you so angry? I'm the one expecting the baby!'

Luke controlled himself with visible effort. 'Come,' he said, taking her by the hand. 'Let us sit down and talk like reasonable people.'

'By all means.' Isobel let him lead her to the sofa. She curled up in a corner and waved Luke to the chair.

He looked so overpoweringly male in her feminine room Isobel's heart started thumping again as his eyes locked with hers.

'If,' he began, 'I had not come here to see you, would you have told me about the child? Ever?'

'I don't know,' she said honestly. 'I intended to wait until after she arrived and see how I felt.'

His eyebrows rose. 'You know it is a girl?'

'Not officially. I just feel it in my bones.'

There was silence for a while. 'It is a bad thing for a child to grow up without a father,' he said at last. 'I have experience of this.'

As Isobel well knew. She sat still, waiting for him to go on.

'We must marry,' he said at last.

Oh, must we? 'No,' she said flatly.

Luke sprang up to loom over her. 'You cannot say no this time, Isobel. We have another life to consider, not just yours, or mine.'

She glared up at him. 'Are you seriously expecting me to marry you and acknowledge you as the father of a child you don't believe is yours, Lukas Andreadis?'

'I know the child is mine,' he said impatiently. 'Are you going to make me pay for the rest of our lives, and our child's life, because I am human, and in my shock I said words I regretted the moment they were uttered?'

'They hurt, Luke.' Isobel hugged her arms across her chest. 'Not least because, before I knew about the baby, I was going to put a different proposition to you when the six weeks were up.'

'What was it?' he said quickly.

'I didn't fancy being some sort of playmate you visited when you had time to spare—'

'It would not have been like that!'

'That's how it seemed to me. Anyway, I was going to suggest that we just lived together, as people do. In your apartment in Athens, or your house in Thessaloniki, or wherever. In basic terms, I wanted to share all your life, not just small doses of it, Luke.'

He gazed down at her in disbelief. 'Is this true?'

'Yes.'

He drew in a deep, unsteady breath. 'If you had, I would have agreed with much enthusiasm after several weeks apart from you. So what changed your mind?'

Isobel patted her stomach. 'I found out about her. I couldn't come asking to live with you once I found I was pregnant.'

'Why not?'

'You would have thought that was the only reason for my

suggestion. Besides, I was afraid you might question my baby's parentage. And I was right,' she added with rancour.

'I refuse to believe that you would be cruel enough to keep our child from me.'

Isobel's heart did a little skip at the 'our'. 'I suppose not,' she said quietly.

Luke raised her hand to his lips and kissed the palm. 'Our child was conceived in love, *ne*? So he—'

'She!'

He laughed unsteadily. 'So it is only right that our child should grow up secure in the love of parents who are husband and wife.'

'That's emotional blackmail,' she protested thickly.

'Call it what you wish. But you must agree, Isobel. We have both suffered from the lack of family in our lives. If you marry me, you will never suffer such lack again.' He gave her the rare smile that always stopped her heart. 'You cannot fight fate, *kardia mou.*'

Luke drew her to her feet with infinite care, his eyes intent on hers, and with a deep, shuddering sigh Isobel surrendered to his arms as his mouth met hers in a kiss that went on and on until neither could breathe. Luke picked her up and sat down with her in his lap, cradling her close.

'Tell me you love me, Isobel,' he commanded thickly.

She gave an unsteady little chuckle. 'There you go, ordering me about as usual. Not that it matters because I do love you, Lukas Andreadis.'

His eyes blazed. 'Then why did you put me through hell? When I read your letter I was like a madman. You did not give your address, and you told me you had destroyed your phone. Andres saved my sanity, Isobel, when he suggested a way to trace you.'

Her lashes were suddenly wet with tears. 'I wasn't doing too well in the sanity department myself. Hormones. I really thought it was the right thing to do at the time.'

Luke smoothed a hand over her hair. 'But now the right thing is very obvious to both of us, *ne*? Even though you never wished for marriage, I swear I will make ours happy for you!'

'But you never fancied marriage either!'

He bent his head to kiss her. 'Then I met you, *agapi mou*, and changed my mind.'

'But you asked me to be your mistress—'

'Lover, not mistress,' he said with tender violence. 'I was afraid you would never agree to marriage, Isobel. I was trying to keep you with me in the way I thought you would like best.'

Her stomach gave a sudden audible rumble and they both laughed.

'Was that my baby saying hello to Papa?' said Luke in a tone which brought a lump to Isobel's throat.

She gave him a wobbly little smile. 'I think she was telling me to say yes this time!'

Normally, Isobel enjoyed the short helicopter flight to Chyros, but this time she sent up a prayer of thanks as Luke set the machine down behind the Villa Medusa.

'Are you all right?' he said tightly as he helped Isobel out.

'Fine,' she lied, managing a smile as Eleni and Spiro came hurrying to meet them.

There was a flurry of greetings, then Eleni frowned as Isobel caught her breath on the way into the house. 'It has started?'

'I think so,' said Isobel through her teeth.

'What did you say?' demanded Luke, catching up with them.

'Your daughter has decided it's her birthday.'

Luke swore long and volubly, his face haggard as he helped

her up the stairs to the master bedroom they shared. 'I should not have given in to you. We should have stayed in reach of the hospital in Athens.'

'Not a chance,' she panted. 'I wanted our child born here on Chyros, like her father.'

And twelve hours later, by which time Isobel was exhausted and Luke demented, their child came into the world protesting loudly. Dr Riga shook Luke's hand in congratulation as Nurse Pappas passed the tightly wrapped bundle to Eleni, who proudly handed it over to Isobel.

'You took your time,' she told her baby drowsily when she was alone with a very pale, haggard husband. She smiled as Luke knelt on the bed to kiss her. 'Isn't she beautiful, darling?'

'Almost as beautiful as you, *hriso mou*,' he said huskily, and smiled as he touched a finger to the baby's cheek. 'But our child is a boy, Isobel. We have a son, not a daughter.'

She stared at him blankly. 'Are you sure?'

Luke nodded, laughing. 'He is most definitely male.'

'Just like his papa.' She chuckled weakly. She cuddled the little bundle to her breast, smiling down into the crumpled sleeping face. 'Oh, well, son, we'll just have to try for a sister next time.'

'*No!*' Luke shook his head vehemently. 'No next time. Ever.' He raised her hand to his lips and kissed it passionately. 'I could not bear it.'

'You don't have to bear it. I do that part.'

'I am not joking!' he said sternly and bent to kiss her. 'I must go. Nurse Pappas says there are things to be done for both of you. Is there something you need first, *glykia mou*?'

'A huge pot of tea and my phone, please,' said Isobel promptly.

'You may have the tea, but I shall ring Joanna and Alyssa

myself, also Andres, who can spread the word in Athens.' He smiled proudly. 'It is the father's privilege, *ne*?'

Her sleepy blue eyes fastened on his. 'Are you proud of your son, Lukas Andreadis?'

'I do not have the vocabulary to say exactly how much, though I would have been just as proud of a daughter,' he assured her and stroked her hair. 'But I am most proud of my wife. You did not complain once.'

She laughed unsteadily. 'No breath to spare for complaints. Besides, all women go through the same process, Luke.'

'But I am not married to other women. Only to you, Isobel.' He smiled as the baby stirred. 'What name shall we give our son?'

She stared at him blankly. 'I was so settled on Olympia for a girl, I never thought about boy names.'

'What was your father's name?'

'Paul. Is there a Greek version?'

'Pavlos. But Paul is used also.' Luke nodded in approval. 'I like that. It sounds good.'

'Now I have given you a son, Lukas Andreadis, I would like something in return,' she said, surprising him.

'Anything your heart desires,' he said huskily and stroked her damp hair. 'What do you want, *hriso mou*?'

'When we've both recovered from this, I want to give a party here to celebrate Paul's birth—and to send your grandfather an invitation.'

Luke eyed her in shock. 'You ask me this at a time when you know I can't refuse, *ne*?'

'That's right.' Isobel smiled at him lovingly. 'You said anything my heart desires, and I desire this very much, darling.'

He sighed heavily. 'Then of course I shall agree. After all, it is not so great a thing. He may not come.' He bent to kiss her gently. 'And now I must go. While Nurse Pappas and Eleni are making you comfortable I shall offer Dr Riga a brandy in libation to the safe arrival of Paul Andreadis.' Luke turned at the door to smile at her, looking so pleased with himself Isobel blew him a loving kiss. 'But I shall make a secret toast of my own. To fate, who gave me the gift of the most beautiful wife and son in the world.'

Coming Next Month

in **Harlequin Presents**®. Available June 29, 2010.

Coming Next Month

in **Harlequin Presents**® EXTRA. Available July 13, 2010.

HPECNM0610

LARGER-PRINT BOOKS!

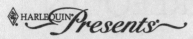

GET 2 FREE LARGER-PRINT
NOVELS PLUS 2 FREE GIFTS!

YES! Please send me 2 FREE LARGER-PRINT Harlequin Presents® novels and my 2 FREE gifts (gifts are worth about $10). After receiving them, if I don't wish to receive any more books, I can return the shipping statement marked "cancel." If I don't cancel, I will receive 6 brand-new novels every month and be billed just $4.55 per book in the U.S. or $5.24 per book in Canada. That's a saving of at least 13% off the cover price! It's quite a bargain! Shipping and handling is just 50¢ per book.* I understand that accepting the 2 free books and gifts places me under no obligation to buy anything. I can always return a shipment and cancel at any time. Even if I never buy another book, the two free books and gifts are mine to keep forever.

176/376 HDN E5NG

Name	(PLEASE PRINT)	
Address		Apt. #
City	State/Prov.	Zip/Postal Code

Signature (if under 18, a parent or guardian must sign)

Mail to the **Harlequin Reader Service:**
IN U.S.A.: P.O. Box 1867, Buffalo, NY 14240-1867
IN CANADA: P.O. Box 609, Fort Erie, Ontario L2A 5X3

Not valid for current subscribers to Harlequin Presents Larger-Print books.

**Are you a subscriber to Harlequin Presents books
and want to receive the larger-print edition?
Call 1-800-873-8635 today!**

* Terms and prices subject to change without notice. Prices do not include applicable taxes. Sales tax applicable in N.Y. Canadian residents will be charged applicable provincial taxes and GST. Offer not valid in Quebec. This offer is limited to one order per household. All orders subject to approval. Credit or debit balances in a customer's account(s) may be offset by any other outstanding balance owed by or to the customer. Please allow 4 to 6 weeks for delivery. Offer available while quantities last.

Your Privacy: Harlequin Books is committed to protecting your privacy. Our Privacy Policy is available online at www.eHarlequin.com or upon request from the Reader Service. From time to time we make our lists of customers available to reputable third parties who may have a product or service of interest to you. If you would prefer we not share your name and address, please check here. ☐

Help us get it right—We strive for accurate, respectful and relevant communications. To clarify or modify your communication preferences, visit us at www.ReaderService.com/consumerschoice.

HPLP10R

HARLEQUIN®

A *Romance*

FOR EVERY MOOD™

Spotlight on

— Heart & Home —

Heartwarming romances
where love can happen
right when you least expect it.

See the next page to enjoy a sneak peek
from Silhouette Special Edition®,
a Heart and Home series.

*Introducing McFARLANE'S PERFECT BRIDE
by* USA TODAY *bestselling author Christine Rimmer,
from Silhouette Special Edition®.*

Entranced. Captivated. Enchanted.

Connor sat across the table from Tori Jones and
couldn't help thinking that those words exactly described
what effect the small-town schoolteacher had on him.
He might as well stop trying to tell himself he wasn't
interested. He was powerfully drawn to her.

Clearly, he should have dated more when he was
younger.

There had been a couple of other women since Jennifer
had walked out on him. But he had never been entranced.
Or captivated. Or enchanted.

Until now.

He wanted her—*her,* Tori Jones, in particular. Not just
someone suitably attractive and well-bred, as Jennifer had
been. Not just someone sophisticated, sexually exciting
and discreet, which pretty much described the two women
he'd dated after his marriage crashed and burned.

It came to him that he…he *liked* this woman. And that
was new to him. He liked her quick wit, her wisdom and
her big heart. He liked the passion in her voice when she
talked about things she believed in.

He liked *her.* And suddenly it mattered all out of
proportion that she might like him, too.

Was he losing it? He couldn't help but wonder. Was
he cracking under the strain—of the soured economy, the
McFarlane House setbacks, his divorce, the scary changes
in his son? Of the changes he'd decided he needed to make
in his life and himself?

Strangely, right then, on his first date with Tori Jones, he didn't care if he just might be going over the edge. He was having a great time—having *fun,* of all things—and he didn't want it to end.

Is Connor finally able to admit his feelings to Tori, and are they reciprocated?
Find out in McFARLANE'S PERFECT BRIDE
by USA TODAY bestselling author Christine Rimmer.
Available July 2010,
only from Silhouette Special Edition®.

Bestselling Harlequin Presents® author

Penny Jordan

brings you an exciting new trilogy...

Needed:
THE WORLD'S MOST
ELIGIBLE
BILLIONAIRES

Three penniless sisters:
how far will they go to save the ones they love?

Lizzie, Charley and Ruby refuse to drown in their debts.
And three of the richest, most ruthless men in the world
are about to enter their lives. Pure, proud but penniless,
how far will these sisters go to save the ones they love?

Look out for

Lizzie's story—**THE WEALTHY GREEK'S
CONTRACT WIFE, July**

Charley's story—**THE ITALIAN DUKE'S
VIRGIN MISTRESS, August**

Ruby's story—**MARRIAGE: TO CLAIM HIS TWINS,**
September

www.eHarlequin.com

HP12927

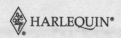

HARLEQUIN®

Showcase

On sale June 8

Reader favorites from the most talented voices in romance

Save $1.00 on the purchase of 1 or more Harlequin® Showcase books.

SAVE $1.00 on the purchase of 1 or more Harlequin® Showcase books.

Coupon expires November 30, 2010. Redeemable at participating retail outlets.
Limit one coupon per customer. Valid in the U.S.A. and Canada only.

52609057

5 65373 00076 2   (8100)0 11654

HSCCOUP0610